ENCHANTED WISHES

THE COMPLETE COLLECTION

VIOLA TEMPEST

VIOLA TEMPEST PUBLISHING

COPYRIGHT

Enchanted Wishes
The Complete Collection

© Copyright 2023 Viola Tempest

Any references to historical events, real people, or real places are used fictitiously. Names, characters, and places are products of the author's imagination.

Cover Design by Evelyne Paniez | www.secretdartiste.be

CONTENTS

DREAMING OF NOELLE

SHATTERED HEART

GAME OF HEARTS

Enchanted WISHES

THE COMPLETE COLLECTION

VIOLA TEMPEST

DREAMING OF NOELLE

ENCHANTED WISHES COLLECTION

Dreaming of NOELLE

of

ENCHANTED WISHES COLLECTION

VIOLA TEMPEST

PROLOGUE

If only I'd known. If only I hadn't been so naïve. So stupid and naïve! Thinking someone like me could ever be with someone like her... well, not again, anyway. I did have it all, once, but then it disappeared as soon as it came into my life. Such a fool. Such a fool.

The days get colder and colder here in this cabin, the nights almost unbearable. Why'd I think living a life in the North Pole of Fairbanks, Alaska was ever a good idea? Such an idiot! I've never been a fan of the cold.

Ever since I graduated from a prestigious university in the north, I'd gone as south as south could get. Texas was a good choice for a while, but even that soon got to be too chilly, and I hauled my ass over to Arizona, where my parents live. Smart. Hell, if Death Valley allowed occupants, I might've just moved there, too. And Erica always came along for the ride, hating the cold just as much as I did.

But that's all just a passing thought now, a memory that will forever stay just a memory. With no transportation, a fallen dream, and a girlfriend I'll never see again, I've lost hope in ever trying to get out of here. Sigh, this is my home now, this cold wooden abyss that's barely able to hold itself up against the angry, raging winds, let alone an entire human being residing in it.

But honestly, if I could go back in time and take it all back, make sure I don't go down the path that I did, I'm not so sure I would. She was everything, my Christmas miracle, and I'd give anything to have her back in my arms.

I turn around and look behind me, sighing again. Guess I'll need more firewood soon, but what's the point anymore?

It's rough enough venturing out there in the dead of winter, risking frostbite to gather frozen wood in my arms. But even so, I'll only just be prolonging my own death. This suffering gets unbearable most of the time, and I don't know how much more I can take. Many nights, I try to close my eyes, try to bring back the image of the girl who once was, but for some reason, she doesn't return. She doesn't seem to ever return.

The rose on my desk, the very same rose I'd given to her the day we became official, I'll never forget. It's the only thing I have left that reminds me of her, and no way in hell am I going to let that just crumple also, much like my heart. She promised me a lifetime of happiness, living together forever, my wish finally coming true.

And of course, I had to be so naïve. I had to trust every pair of walking heel who came in my direction and flashed me a smile. The same thing happened with Erica, and the same thing is happening now.

So, why do I keep trying to convince myself that Noelle's different? That she's not like Erica. That's she's sweet and genuine, that she truly loves me for me. Why do I keep holding onto the hope that she'll come back, that she really is my Christmas miracle? Why can't I just let go?

I used to love the holidays, especially Christmas. The chimes of carolers singing. The bells of mistletoes ringing. The harmonious laughter of joyful children as they danced around the brightly decorated tree in front of City Hall. And it didn't matter to me one bit that there was never any snow. I did live in a desert, after all, the lukewarm temperature giving off a summer vibe rather than a winter one. But nope, didn't matter to me one bit.

I had everything I needed, with or without the snow and

frigid winter. My career was finally kicking off. My brother just had a baby, and Erica and I were due to have one soon, too. My mother almost had a heart attack when we told her Erica was carrying.

"Before you're married?!" she gasped and pretended to fall over in her usual overdramatic fashion.

But Dad was always there to catch her, right before her head hit anything beside the throw pillows. Sometimes I wonder whether they'd still be together if he'd let her fall once, just once. Probably not. Mom's overdramatic, but she's also the most ruthless person I'd ever met in my entire life, and I'm not just saying that because she's my mother.

The year was 2018, that was going to be my best Christmas ever. Wanna know why? It was the year I finally asked Erica to be, not only the mother of my child, but also my wife. She'd been hinting at it for a while. I could read her like a book. She'd been texting her girlfriends for the past several months, going out late with them and coming home at wee hours in the morning. I knew it was because she'd wanted to get their opinions on how long it'd take me before I finally popped the question. They were all married, after all. It just made sense.

I knew. Like I said, I could read her like a book... or so I thought.

That look she gave me when I got down on one knee and popped the question was one I will never be able to get out of my head. A look of pure disgust, like she was completely fine with having my baby but wanted to hurl at the thought of having to look at my face every day. Women, can't live with them, and they certainly didn't want to live with me.

Turns out, all those hints I'd been getting weren't hints to propose. They were hints to break up. All those nights she'd spent texting her girlfriends and going out with them for advice, she'd been seeing some guy named Milton behind my back. A co-worker, she'd tried to pass off as at first, but it didn't take long before I found out that she'd met him at my brother's baby shower. What the hell kind of name is Milton, anyway? The curses just never stop coming, do they? Just my luck.

And there she went. Packed up the little suitcase that she had and walked right out the door... the morning of Christmas day. Christmas hadn't been the same since. Two more had gone by, and that Christmas spirit I'd been so fond of, right out the door and straight into a fire pit. By the time the third one rolled around, my friends and family had grown sick of me.

"Just get over her already," they'd say to me. "It's been three fucking years. Just get over her and move on."

If you haven't guessed it, that only added fuel to my anger. For six years, we'd been together, Freshman year in college and dating ever since. Not to mention that she had my own flesh and blood sitting inside that filthy womb of hers... at least, I hope that was my child. What did it matter anymore? She was gone... off to batshit nowhere, and that restraining order she'd gotten against me certainly didn't help in me trying to find her.

But I still tried. I still loved her. Of course, I did. For nearly three years, I continued trying to bring her back into my life, looking her up on the Internet and bugging the hell out of friends. I'd be lucky if I found someone to help me. Most of them just shut me out, saying I was bringing them down and ruining their holiday spirit. The hypocrisy. Others, the rare few, only agreed to help me if I got the hell out of their homes. But even still, I never found her. She's out there somewhere with my child, and there's no way I can get in touch with her.

"Will you snap out of it?" My brother, Mark, yelled over in my direction and tossed a few popcorn kernels at me.

The year was now 2021, and those few weeks before Christmas changed my life forever.

I picked up the kernels, ate a couple, and tossed the rest back over at him. "Dude, stop! You're wasting food!" I exclaimed.

But he just shrugged. "Eh, the dog will take care of it. He's a garbage disposal. It's why we named him that."

"It's why *you* named him that. Mom and Dad named him Rufus, remember?"

"Yeah." Mark shrugged. "But that name's dumb. I like Garbage much, much better."

I rolled my eyes at him and reached over to the tree to pluck off a candy cane. I figured the more I ate, the less there'd be left when the actual day rolled around. Plus, it didn't hurt that I also have a sweet tooth when it comes to peppermint.

"Of course, you would. He's the animal equivalent of you. I'm surprised Shanna doesn't hide the food so you wouldn't eat it all."

"Mom! Max's being an asshole again!" he called out to our mother, who was making chili in the kitchen.

"Settle down, boys," she said on autopilot. Then she stepped out into the living room, the garlic-coated ladle still in her hand, sauce slowly dripping onto the hardwood floor. "You two are grown men. I didn't invite you over here for lunch just so you can throw popcorn at each other. Now, clean up the mess. Chili's ready."

Mark watched as Mom walked back into the kitchen, then turned around and stuck his tongue out at me, as if he'd just won. I grumbled back at him and walked into the kitchen to help Mom, snagging a taste of the first scoop before he had a chance to. That was usually my way of getting revenge.

Things didn't get much easier as the days went by. The

closer and closer we got to Christmas, the more bitter I became. All around me, including the office, restaurants, and parks, everyone was starting to get into that holiday spirit, with their tinsel and billions of ornaments. I wanted to vomit. The cheerfulness and colorful lights gave me an even bigger migraine than the one I had the day Erica walked out. It was all just so… so… sickening.

When I walked into the office twelve days before, everyone was already dressed in ugly green and red sweaters, getting drunk on the eggnog in their hands, and handing out Santa hats for everyone else to get into that festive mood. I grabbed one, sat down at my desk, and threw it in the trash. I didn't want any part in the celebration. The eggnog, I did drink, however; the chilled liquid running down my throat was enough to ease my anxiety for a time being. Anything I could do to make this awful month pass by that much faster was a good thing, in my opinion.

"Ho! Ho! Ho!" my boss, Peter Sands, said as he came over to my desk.

I could smell the stench of eggnog on his breath, the egg whites coating the mustache on his upper lip, and the cinnamon powder blowing from his mouth whenever he coughed. Disgusting. I tried to turn my body away so none of it would get on me, but turned out that it didn't matter. Most of it didn't reach past the belly of his white dress shirt and paisley tie. Those, paired with his thick framed glasses, showed the man's true lack of style. But then again, it didn't' seem like he had anyone in his life to tell him otherwise.

"Mr. Miller," he continued. "You know, being antisocial isn't going to get you bonus points with the boss, especially not when your boss is the life of the party."

"Sorry, sir. I'm not being antisocial. I just have a lot of work to get done."

But Peter wouldn't have it. He pushed back my chair and

sat his lard of an ass down on my desk, smacked on top of the notebook I was writing in.

"Nope!" he chimed. "Today, your job is to join the party and have fun!" Then his jolly smile turned into a cold, death glare. "Do it, or you're fired," followed by another jolly laugh. "I'm just messing with you. Come! Join the others. Grab a slice of cake. Enjoy yourself!"

It all seemed so innocent, but I knew what he was trying to do. Steer me away from my work so he could berate me later for not getting everything done. It's one of the cruelest tricks in the book.

"No, thanks," I shook my head and said again. "I have a lot of work to do."

He let out a vociferous laugh, then patted me on the back. "Ha! Suit yourself, party pooper."

Four agonizing hours later, I was finally able to get into my car and drive home. It would've taken an army to squeeze past the drunk crowd blocking the entire front entrance. But it didn't bother me… especially not when I was so desperate that the fire exit seemed like the much better option. They'd deal with the alarm after I was long gone. Didn't need me.

When I finally got home, I threw my briefcase on top of my couch, the remote that was resting there bouncing off and onto the floor.

"Whatever," I muttered, then proceeded into the kitchen to have my own party, a pack of cigarettes and a bottle of whiskey.

It's all I needed lately. Mark tried to set me up every now and then, the next gold digger always worse than the last, and it got to the point where I'd just roll my eyes, get their number, and never reach out. They're all the same, just another heartbreaker, much like Erica.

The nights alone had been getting harder and harder lately. I'd debated getting a puppy, something to keep me company, but with my luck, it'd just leave me, too. My shitty unlovable life.

When the butt of the cigarette went out, I downed the rest of my whiskey. When that was finished… what then?

Angrily, I smashed the glass bottle against my balcony, glass shards spilling across the ground, and then held the jagged edges to my wrist. I could do it. One swift motion, and the hell I was living in would all be over. No one would ever need to know. Not like anyone ever visited. And even if they did find out, who cares? I'd be dead anyway.

The glass moved closer toward my bare arm, veins popping and forehead sweating.

"Just one swift motion," I kept telling myself, but the more I tried to push, the more my body resisted.

Finally, the anxiety became too overwhelming, and I threw the remaining half of the bottle off my balcony, hearing it shatter on the street of downtown Phoenix before retreating into my room and climbing into bed.

"Maybe tomorrow will be better."

It usually never was.

2

"Max, Max, wake up."

My eyes sprung open to the sound of a female voice. "Huh? Who's there?"

But at first glance, I found that I was no longer in my own room, nor in my own apartment. The plain white walls that I had been so used to had suddenly transformed into ones of crimson red that surrounded a room of holiday decorations. At first, I thought I'd been kidnapped. That my dad or brother had come into my apartment in the middle of the night and dragged me out to celebrate Christmas with them.

But when the female voice walked out, I'd nearly shit my pants.

"Erica?" I asked. "Why are you here? I never thought I'd see you again."

My brain felt as though it was spinning in circles. I'd spent years chasing down my ex, with no luck, and suddenly, she was standing in a vomit-inducing room wearing a Santa hat and carrying a platter full of chocolate chip cookies.

The woman smiled at me. The way her freshly-painted lips curved upwards reminded me of why I'd fallen in love with Erica in the first place. But then she spoke, and my brain spun even more.

"No, Max. I'm Noelle, and I'm glad I finally found you," the woman said.

I'd nearly shit my pants again at the disbelief. It couldn't be. Erica never mentioned a sister, much less a twin. I shook my head. No, I would've known if she had one. I knew everything about her... well, almost everything. Milton. Fuck him.

"Who... who are you?" I managed to stutter. "Where... where am I?"

I carefully backed away as she inched closer. The plastic ornaments and fake snow strewn over the living room floor definitely made it harder than it needed to be. And even as I stumbled into a corner, she continued closing in, finally reaching down and placing a hand on my knee.

I couldn't stop staring. The resemblance to Erica. It was uncanny, like she'd been reincarnated from the woman herself, the woman who was still alive.

She giggled, the serious look on her face turning bubbly within seconds. "Silly duckling," she whispered, her voice sweet and angelic.

Duckling? I thought. *That's what Erica used to call me.*

"Who are you?" I demanded again, my tone still clearly not strong enough to scare her away.

"Silly, I'm Noelle. I just told you!" She giggled again.

"I don't see what's so funny."

Her cheeks blushed red, as if I'd embarrassed her somehow, the smile on her face gone.

"I'm sorry. You're just so cute when you're confused. I didn't mean to laugh at you." She leaned in and gave me a kiss on the cheek. My body tingled at the feeling of her touch, as if it were reacting to it. "I'm Noelle," she whispered again. "And I've been looking everywhere for you."

BUZZ!

The sound of my alarm clock startled me, and I nearly fell out of bed. When I finally regained my composure, I found myself back in my disgustingly plain room. The tree, the ornaments, the fake snow, the red walls, they were all gone. I turned my head from side to side. And Noelle, she was nowhere to be found.

It must've just been a dream. I really should lay off that whiskey.

My head was pounding when I rolled out of bed. I fumbled with my alarm clock until I figured out how to shut it off. And when I finally got a chance to take a good look at it, I saw the date. Great. Eleven days before Christmas.

I'd been dreading Christmas this year. My mother said she'd found someone, the daughter of a neighbor she thought would make a perfect wife for me. And if I didn't at least meet her, she'd disown me. I knew she was kidding, but the woman wasn't getting any younger, and I figured I owed her at least that much.

But I couldn't get Noelle out of my head. That dream had felt so real, the touch of her delicate fingers so natural that it felt like I was living two lives: the one I dreaded in reality, and the one I craved in my dream. It still didn't make any sense to me. To this day, I don't think it'll ever make sense to me, why she looked so similar to Erica. All I knew was, I had to see her again.

That night, I sat out on my balcony and smoked a cigarette, followed by a bottle of whiskey. I needed to repeat exactly what I did the night before if I had any chance of seeing Noelle again. I needed to find out more, who she was, and why she had suddenly decided to make an appearance in my life.

When my nerves finally settled, and I fell asleep, I found myself sitting in that same room, obnoxiously decorated with sparkling tinsel and stockings hanging on the walls. There was a glass of eggnog sitting on the coffee table, and I lifted it up to take a sip. Delicious! The best eggnog I'd ever had in my entire life.

"Do you like it?" Noelle startled me when she walked in, holding a small box wrapped in snowflake wrapping paper with a large red bow on top.

"Uh huh," I managed to get out, the liquid still in my mouth as I struggled not to choke.

She smiled. "I'm glad."

Then she sat down beside me on the red velvet couch, and I could smell the sweet aroma of perfume she had on her body. She smelled like an angel sent down from Heaven, and I felt like I had died.

"This is for you," she said, handing me the present.

"For me?" I asked, confused. "But it's not Christmas yet."

She giggled. "I know. Just open it."

I grabbed the box from her delicate hands, our fingers touching in the process and sending a shiver of tingles up and down my body. She continued to look at me as I opened it, my face blushing at the embarrassment. Inside the neatly wrapped box, which I had torn open like a hungry beast, was a wrist watch.

"Wow!" I exclaimed. "Is this really for me?"

She nodded, her smile growing larger. "Read the back."

I turned the watch around, and engraved on the back were the words: Max and Noelle Forever.

"I... I don't understand," I said to her, turning my body in her direction.

"You will... soon enough."

The sound of my alarm blared again, and this time, I did fall out of bed. December 16th. Another day, another shitty day. I looked down at my wrist, expecting the dream to stay a dream, but right there, decorating my left wrist, was the same watch Noelle had just given me.

I didn't know what was happening, with my dream, with Noelle. But the more I saw her, the more I felt pulled to her. And none of it made any sense, the strange tie between fantasy and reality. Who was she? And how'd a gift I'd received in my dream appear in reality? I questioned it at first, tempted to call the cops and tell them someone's been sneaking into my apartment through a dream, but I was pretty sure they'd just laugh at me. A magical watch given to me by someone in my dream? It was crazy for *me* to even think it. But soon, as the days continued to go by, I stopped questioning it. I stopped trying to fight it. Noelle truly *was* the best thing that had ever happened to me, and I couldn't risk anything that would ruin that.

Every night for the next seven nights, I continued to repeat my patterns of behavior, anxiously rushing through the day just so I could down that bottle of whiskey and fall asleep to see her. I started to grow closer and closer to Noelle, not just physically, but it felt as if our brains just connected. It was as if she *was* Erica, but a hundred times better. It felt strange to think at the time, but I had fallen in love with her.

And on that seventh day, two days before Christmas, we finally kissed. To be honest, I'd wanted to kiss her on day two, but I didn't want to scare her away. She was just so perfect, and after what had happened with Erica, I didn't think I'd ever fall in love again. For the past three years, I'd had it in my plans to simply die alone, with or without a dog. I hadn't decided yet, but definitely not with a woman.

"You have no idea how much I've wanted to do that," I said to her when I gently pushed away.

We were both standing by the beautifully decorated tree, the twinkling lights brightening my day and bringing back the joy I used to have when it came to Christmas. The music playing on the radio lifted the terrible mood I'd been in during work that day, and the sparkling tinsel against the reflection of the chandelier no longer made me want to puke.

"I do know," she replied. "Because I've wanted to do the same ever since I first saw you. We belong together, Max. You and I. This is destiny."

"It is. It really, really is." I leaned in to kiss her again, my hands wrapping around her waist and pulling her body close to mine.

I'd never noticed it before, but her body was no less than a perfect twenty, and when she pressed against me, it felt like we completed a puzzle.

It felt as if my life was finally complete.

3

uzz! I woke up to the sound of my alarm, falling out of bed once again. But instead of the frustration that usually came after, I was happy. I was actually happy to be alive. I now had something worth living for. And that something was Noelle. I eagerly jumped out of bed and skipped into the shower, brushing my teeth while humming to Jingle Bells. Tomorrow was finally Christmas, and I couldn't wait to spend it with Noelle.

"You look chipper today," my co-worker, Steve, said to me when I walked into the office.

I had a steaming hot cup of cocoa in my hand and Noelle's Santa hat perched on top of my head, still humming the same song.

"I am," I said with a grin as I threw my briefcase on top of my desk.

"Care to share?"

"I met someone. A girl."

I originally had no intention of telling anyone about Noelle, afraid that they'd think I had gone crazy, but I felt so ecstatic that I could no longer keep it to myself. I winced as soon as those words left my mouth, and prepared myself for jabs and ridicules, the works. For the past three years, I'd gone on and on about never dating again, swearing off women and relationships forever, that I would never again let some broad dictate my life and change it. And now, here I was, grinning like a monkey getting its butt scratched and skipping down the halls of the office.

"Congrats, man," Steve said instead, patting me on the back. "It's 'bout time you get back on the market. We were all rooting for you." He perched himself on top of my desk. "So, who's the lucky gal? Anyone I know?"

I glared at him. "Anyone you know? Does it look like we know the same people?"

He shrugged. "No, but it never hurts to ask. The world's a lot smaller than you think."

I shook my head. So wrong. His words were so wrong, in so many ways.

"Her name's Noelle. We've been seeing each other for about two weeks now, and we had our first kiss last night. It's going pretty well. And no, it's *not* someone you know."

"She hot? Any hot friends? Come on, man. I need details!"

"Why?"

"Because…," he said smoothly, "if you ever get dumped by this one too, I'd like to know what my chances are."

"Get the fuck out of here." I rolled my eyes and pushed him over.

But for the rest of the day, I couldn't stop thinking about what he'd said. I mean, Noelle *was* hot. But that also meant there was a high chance of her leaving me, just like Erica did. I'll admit, I'm not the most handsome man in the world, but I treat women right, and that's what I'd been priding myself on. But then again, Erica left, so it clearly hadn't been working.

I grew more and more anxious over the course of that day. The thought of losing the girl of my dream to another man was too unbearable to even think about. I wasn't even sure if I ever got over Erica, the person I thought was my forever; I'd simply replaced her with Noelle. If I were to lose her too, I wasn't sure what I'd do with myself.

Then I chuckled at my thoughts. Why was I so worried about losing her? She lived in my dream, a figment of my imagination. However strange that dream had been, mixing with reality, there's no way she could leave me. It was impossible!

That night, I lied in bed with her present in my hands and fell asleep. I'd gotten her a diamond bracelet, carved with our initials on it. If she was able to give me a watch through my dream, I didn't see why I wouldn't be able to give her a bracelet through reality. And to top it off, I had attached a single rose on top, a single rose to signify our love for each other.

It didn't take long before I found myself back in that room, that red-walled room covered in tinsel and stockings. But I was happy to see them. Christmas was only a few hours away, and I was excited for the chance to spend it with Noelle.

But she didn't show up. After two hours of sitting on that red velvet couch, my best iron-pressed suit beginning to crease, she still didn't show. I didn't understand. I did everything the same, a cigarette, whiskey, even forced myself to smash the glass bottle and hold it against my wrist, so why wasn't she here?

Maybe she's just running late, I foolishly thought to myself. *She'll show. I know she will.*

Four hours had passed, and I still stupidly held that gift box on my lap. I couldn't even smell the freshly-baked cookies or eggnog that she usually had ready for me. But still, I continued to sit there, waiting and waiting for her, a smile still resting on my face. It wasn't like I could leave, even if I wanted to. But I didn't. I kept telling myself that she'd show. Just waiting. Waiting. Waiting.

BUZZ!

My alarm rang the next morning, Christmas Day, and I woke up in my own bed, with the boring white sheets. The single red rose and ugly wrapped gift box had both fallen onto the floor when I rolled over in the middle of the night.

Just my luck. I finally found a woman I wanted to spend my life with, and of course, she'd left, just like all the others. I was devastated! Hate began to boil in my blood, and I threw the gift into the trash before throwing my sheets off my body. I stormed into the living room, which I had neatly decorated with whatever last-minute trinkets and a fake plastic tree I managed to get from the dollar store, and threw them all into a trash bag. I didn't want anything to do with Christmas, or Noelle, or anyone, for that matter.

The office was closed for Christmas, giving me an excuse to not leave my apartment. But even if it wasn't, I would've called in sick. I felt as if my heart was breaking. Every day, ever since I first met Noelle, I started to believe that there was hope in my life again, that things were finally going to turn around for me. I'd even joined in on holiday conversations in the office and bought several gifts for my nephew. Now, they sat in the same trash bag as the rest of the useless junk.

My phone dinged, and a message from Mark popped up, asking me when I'd arrive at our parents for Christmas lunch. I immediately deleted his message and threw my phone across the room. Fat chance in hell was I gonna go over now. Everything was ruined, and it was all Noelle's fault. I hated her! Why'd she have to come into my life if she was just going to walk right back out?

My phone dinged again, then once more, but I ignored it and went into the kitchen to grab a pack of cigarettes and a bottle of whiskey. After Erica left me, I'd stocked up on more whiskey than I'd ever need in a lifetime. But it didn't bother me. Can never have too many. And as I walked back out, I picked up a knife.

Sitting out on my balcony, under the blinding sun, and listening to the sickening sound of laughing children out on the street, I took several swigs from the bottle and leaned back with a cigarette in my mouth. Time to feel sorry for myself again. I didn't know what I had done wrong in my life to deserve all this. My heart was barely even healed before it had gotten broken again. I was only twenty-five, but I'd felt like I'd experienced enough pain for a lifetime.

The knife. I didn't bring it out for no reason. While everyone else was too busy celebrating a holiday that had turned into pure greed, I was suffering alone. And I liked it that way. Less messy, and less to explain.

"I loved you, Noelle. Why didn't you just fucking show up?"

Tears continued to pour down my cheeks as the knife came closer to my wrist. I was really going to do it this time.

I was really done with all these games. No more. I'd had enough.

Suddenly, my doorbell rang, pulling me away from my plan. Grumbling, I knew it had to be Mark, or my mom, or someone else who had come to throw their happiness in my face. I didn't want to answer. I just wanted to end it right there, the pain too overwhelming to bear. But what if it was important? What if someone in my family had an accident, and I'd chosen to off myself instead?

The bell rang again while I paced back and forth with my thoughts. Eventually giving in, I put the knife down to go answer it.

"Don't go anywhere," I said to the knife. "I'll be back."

I was still in my pajamas, baggy stained sweats and an old T-shirt, but whatever, it wasn't like I had anyone to impress. The bell rang once more.

"Hold on!" I yelled. "Chill the fuck out!"

Kicking aside the phone that had been thrown, I swung open the door, and my jaw dropped.

4

" Merry Christmas, Max Miller!"

I couldn't believe it. Sitting outside, on top of the hood of my car, and dressed in the most adorable Christmas outfit, was Noelle. Could it really be? I blinked and pinched myself several times, but the sting assured me that this wasn't a dream. She was really here. Noelle was really here! Live, in person, sitting outside my apartment.

All this time, I thought she was only part of my dream.

Never did I ever wonder whether she really existed. I mean, it made sense. The touch of her body felt so real... so did her breath against my ear, and... and the watch! I didn't care how. I didn't care why. I didn't care that just minutes before, I hated her.

Tears of joy welled in my eyes, and I ran over to embrace her in my arms. She felt so real, like she had felt when I first held her. I felt the warmth beginning to come back inside my chest, my heart beating faster and faster as she pressed against me and snuggled her nose in my neck. I didn't want to let go. I didn't ever want to let go. Ever. My neighbors all stared at me like I was a lunatic, but I didn't care. All I cared about was the woman in my arms.

"Max, I—" She started to speak, but I pressed my lips against hers and interrupted whatever she was going to say.

None of that matter at this moment. I wanted to kiss her, taste her, make up for all the lost hours we could've spent together. My frustration toward her absence had disappeared. Her lips felt so warm and soothing against mine that I wanted to kiss her forever.

When I finally pulled away, five long minutes later, my arms were still wrapped around her. I still feared that as soon as I let go, she'd disappear again, and I couldn't have that. Not again. My heart couldn't handle another one.

"Max, I—" She started to speak again.

"I love you!" I blurted out, interrupting her once again.

But she didn't get mad. Instead, she threw her arms around my neck and smacked her lips hard against mine.

"I love you too, Max! And I want to apologize for not showing up last night. I was trying to make it a surprise by showing up on your front door instead, for Christmas, to show you that dreams can come true. I hope you're not angry with me."

I had been angry, but I wasn't going to tell her that. It

wasn't like telling her would make me feel any better. It'd just make both of us feel that much worse.

I shook my head and smiled at her. "I'm not angry with you at all. I love you so much."

The sun was starting to melt the snowfall from the night before. It was rare for Arizona to gather so much snow, something that only happened once every few years, but despite the chilly air that brushed against my cold skin, I loved that it was a White Christmas, a perfect Christmas.

My body shivered, suddenly realizing how cold it actually was. "Let's go inside," I told her, leading her inside with one arm still around her waist.

I didn't let go of her when we walked through the front door and into the living room. I didn't let go of her until I led her into my bedroom and laid her down on top of my sheets, and then climbed over her to kiss her even more. I wasn't sure what had possessed me. I wasn't usually like this, so forward, usually shyer and more reserved when it came to women. But with Noelle, I felt like she'd been mine for years, the lust that I had toward her so overpowering that I didn't want to stop until I felt myself inside her.

"I love you, Noelle, I love you so fucking much." I pulled off her Santa hat and ruffled my fingers through her chestnut brown hair, and then slid my fingers down to the zipper of her boots and undid them. When my fingers finally made their way back up, they went slowly, grazing up and down her bare legs before reaching up her upper thigh and under her short dress.

She didn't hesitate. Unlike Erica when we made love for the first time, Noelle didn't hesitate, as if we'd done this many times before.

The next twenty minutes was the most pleasurable moment of my entire life thus far. Our bodies intertwined between my sheets, and she whispered her moans in my ear as I gently gestured my hip between her legs. She was fragile, a snow globe I never wanted to break, and when I finished, so did she, our two bodies becoming one.

"That was amazing," I sighed when we separated and had our backs against the bed. Her head was resting on my bare chest, and I continued to run my fingers through her hair.

"Best feeling ever," she chimed. "Do you know that you're my first?"

"No kidding! Really?" Hearing her say that made this moment that much more special.

"Yes." She nodded. "And I want you to be my only."

Before I could respond, my doorbell rang again. This time, I was sure it someone coming to fetch me for Christmas lunch.

"I'll be right back," I said, kissing her on the forehead and throwing my clothes on.

When I swung open the door, Mark was standing there with his wife, Shanna.

"What the hell, man? Why you screening my calls? I've been trying to reach you all morning."

"Sorry." I rubbed the back of my neck. It felt like someone was running their fingers up and down it, but no one was behind me. "I couldn't find my phone."

"You mean that phone?" Mark pointed to the spot beside my feet, where the screen of my phone had slightly cracked from when I threw it.

"Uh… yeah… I guess."

"And why do you have so many garbage bags laying around? You know trash day isn't until Wednesday, right?"

"Huh?" I looked around my living room, almost forgetting that I had bagged up all my Christmas decorations. "Yeah… I guess I forgot."

"I swear, sometimes I wonder how you're the smart one in the family." Mark shook his head. "Anyway, Mom and Dad are waiting for you. Everyone's already there. Come on! You can ride with us."

"Actually, I think I'm going to drive myself." I then turned my head around and spotted Noelle's black boots. "And I think I'm gonna bring someone. A girl."

Shanna beamed with happiness, like she was even more excited than I was about this. "Oh my god! You finally did it? You finally got a girlfriend?"

"Yeah, I guess I did."

She threw her arms around me and gave me a quick hug. "I'm so happy for you! Mark keeps saying you'll die alone, but I had faith in you."

"Geez, thanks, babe. Way to sell me out," Mark joked at his wife. Then he turned his attention back to me. "But yeah, man, bring her. I'm sure Mom will love to meet the special chick that captured her favorite son's heart. But make it quick. Everyone's starving!"

"I'll be there in thirty." I saluted him and closed the door.

Noelle was still naked beneath the sheets when I returned. God, she looked more beautiful every time I saw her.

"Who was that?" she asked.

"My brother, Mark." I climbed back into bed and kissed her on the cheek. "How would you like to come with me to my parents for Christmas lunch? The whole family will be there, and I'm sure they'd be thrilled to meet you."

She blushed. "I don't know. What if they don't like me? I don't want them to hate you too for being with me."

"Nah." I kissed her again. "I love you, and I promise you they will, too."

Exactly thirty minutes later, Noelle and I were standing outside my parents' house. I'd fished the presents out from the trash bag and loaded them into the trunk of my car. I looked over at Noelle, who looked perfectly comfortable in her short sleeveless dress, while I was freezing my ass off. I didn't know how she did it. Like the cold didn't even bother her.

It took two rings before Mom swung open the door and greeted me.

"Max! I'm so glad you could make it!" She gave me a hug and a quick peck on the cheek.

I hugged her back. "Thanks for having me, Mom." I gestured over to Noelle, my fingers wrapped around hers. "This is Noelle, my girlfriend."

But instead of another happy grin on her face and a hug for Noelle, her smile turned into a frown, and she looked at me as if I had just grown a tail.

"Come on in! Everyone's waiting!" she said instead, turning her back and walking inside.

That's weird,

I thought. *Why was she so cold to Noelle?*

"I told you no one would like me," Noelle whispered beside me as I led her inside.

But I brushed it off. "Nah, I'm sure it was just a misunderstanding. She's probably stressed out from all the cooking. I'm sure the rest of the family will find you delightful."

We walked into the dining room to find everyone already seated, with two empty chairs remaining for Noelle and I. As we sat down, the rest of the crowd was already digging into their food, so I scooped up a spoonful of mashed potatoes for Noelle, and then one for myself.

"Delicious, Ma, really," I said to my mother, who gave me a nod and tended to my nephew who had spilled gravy all over his nice shirt.

"So, Max," Mark said when he noticed my presence. "Where's this girlfriend of yours? She running late?"

I lowered my brows at him. Was he kidding me? What the

hell's wrong with my family? "Um… she's right next to me?" I pointed over to Noelle, who gave Mark a shy wave.

"Huh? What are you talking about? That's Grandma. Unless you two have something going on that no one else knows about."

I watched as Grandma opened her eyes in horror and quickly shook her head before returning to her potatoes. "No, not Grandma. Noelle, she's literally sitting right next to me. Why are you being so rude?"

That's when Dad sat in the seat beside me… right on top of Noelle.

"Hey, son, I've been meani—"

"Dad! Get off! You're sitting on her!" I jumped up and yelled, pulling my father off my girlfriend.

"Whoa! Whoa! Sorry! I thought that seat was empty."

"What the hell is wrong with all of you?!" I shouted at my family. "After three years, three fucking years, I finally find love again, and you're all acting like assholes! If you don't want to welcome Noelle into the family, then I won't be part of it, either." I grabbed her by the hand. "Come on, Noelle. Let's get out of here."

"Max, wait!" Mom called after me.

"Save it, Mom. I'm done." I slammed the front door behind me and opened the passenger door for Noelle before climbing into the driver's seat and pulling out of the drive-way. Not once did I try to look back.

EPILOGUE

Looking back, I should've seen it as a red flag when Mark said no one was there. My whole family was just looking out for me, concerned about my mental health. But I was too stubborn to believe them, too stubborn to listen to anyone else but myself.

"Let's move," Noelle had said to me during the drive home.

"Move? To where?"

"The North Pole. Alaska. I feel like that's where I belong,

with the cold. I don't like the warm weather here. It makes me feel sad."

Just the thought of having to live somewhere with temperature that dropped down into the negatives sent chills throughout my body. But Noelle meant everything to me, and if she wanted to move to Alaska, then I'd have to suck it up and move there with her.

So, a week later, we loaded our things into my car and headed north, driving for nearly six days before we finally arrived at a beat-up log cabin up in the mountains.

"I used to live here," Noelle said, "when I was just a little girl. It's been so long I almost forgot what it looks like."

I walked around the dilapidated building and took in the sights. There was definitely a musky smell to the place, like it had been left abandoned for decades. It also looked like one swift blow of a blizzard would send the whole place down to the ground. But Noelle seemed so happy, playing in the snow like an innocent child, and I was willing to do anything for her, including fixing up the place as much as I could to make it livable.

That was three weeks ago. Three long weeks before I finally got past my lovesick ways and realized that Noelle wasn't real. That she was never real to begin with. She wasn't real when she appeared at my front door Christmas morning, and she wasn't real when I brought her over to my parents. No wonder no one could see her. She didn't exist. But I'd wanted so much for her to exist that I made myself believe that the person I saw in my dream was a real person.

The first few days after moving into this cabin was just as expected. Happily in love and sharing every moment together. I had enough savings to care for both of us for at least a couple months before I had to venture out and get a job. Sands wasn't thrilled when I mailed my resignation to him while staying at a hotel in Montana. But it had to be done. I had to follow my heart, and that was with Noelle.

But soon, tension started to grow between us. She grew more and more distant as so did I, the cold numbing my brain as much as it was numbing the skin on my body. And two weeks later, I woke up, and she was gone. Not a single word or note was left about where she was going, and there were no signs of where she had gone, as if she had just vanished. That's when I started to see the signs.

Why is it that the one person I finally fall in love with after Erica turns out to be just an illusion? I had wanted Erica back in my life for so long that I somehow created an alternative version of her instead, in the form of Noelle, forcing myself to believe that she could be more than just a dream.

But even now, even as I find myself freezing in this cabin alone, with a rusty immobile vehicle outside and no one to hold for warmth, I still want her back. And I'll do anything to see her again, to hold her again. I'd given up my entire life for this woman, and I'm not about to walk away with nothing.

I finished the last sips of my tea. The supplies I'd brought with me are beginning to either spoil or dwindle, but I didn't care. I'm too burnt out. Placing my mug down, I retreat to my bed, throwing a warm robe over my body and climbing in under the sheets.

Slowly, I close my eyes and let my body fall to sleep.

"Welcome home, Max." And there she is, Noelle, dressed in that same Santa hat and cute little dress she'd always worn, standing in a place that resembles a more picture-perfect version of the cabin I was in.

Lights decorated the crimson red walls. Eggnog and a platter of chocolate chip cookies sat on the glass coffee table. And a large evergreen tree stood by the fireplace, twinkling with tinsel and sparkling lights. I pick up a cookie and walk over to the red velvet couch, sitting down beside my beautiful girlfriend.

"Merry Christmas." I smile, leaning over to kiss her.

The End

SHATTERED HEART

ENCHANTED WISHES COLLECTION

Shattered HEART

ENCHANTED WISHES COLLECTION

VIOLA TEMPEST

1

Chris drummed his fingers on the steering wheel as he waited for the standstill traffic to come back up to a slow crawl. After a grueling day at work, he was eager to get home to his fiancé. He imagined she had dinner prepared for him, as she usually did. As a professional chef, she graced him daily with her decadent, expert meals.

When he finally pulled around the corner into his driveway and stepped through the front door, he found an empty living room. He smelled nothing cooking from the kitchen, and when he wandered in there, he found it empty.

"Leah?" he called out.

He heard the shuffling of rushed footsteps on the stairs and glanced through the living room to find her panting at the bottom of the steps.

"Chris," she said. "You're home early."

Bewilderment knit his brows together. He glanced down at his wristwatch.

"No, I'm not," he said. "I'm ten minutes late."

Leah stared at him expectantly, like he was supposed to say something else. There was a strange contortion on her features, something frazzled and flustered.

"Are you alright?" he pressed, treading through the living room to peer closer at her face. He sensed something amiss.

She nodded and backed away from him as he reached towards her face.

"I'm fine," she said, her words hurried and slurred together. "I'm sorry I lost track of time. Let me get dinner going for you."

She darted around him and slipped into the kitchen. Chris was left standing in the living room alone, listening to the rattling sound of pots and pans in the kitchen. He heard the gas click on the stove and frowned.

Chris had known Leah since they were only fourteen. He knew her well and could tell that something was not right. Concerned, he followed her into the kitchen and came to stand behind her at the stove. His hands fell to her hips, like they had so many times before.

But instead of leaning back into his touch like she usually did, Leah slipped out of the circle of his arms and moved to the kitchen sink.

"Leah, is something bothering you?" he asked, watching

her flit around the kitchen like a bee, wielding knives, stirring pots, and washing vegetables.

She refused to look at him as she bustled around, keeping her head low to her chest. Chris began to feel a sickening, burbling dread sloshing around in his stomach.

"I told you I'm fine, Chris," she insisted.

He gave her a disbelieving look that she did not catch. She continued to ignore him as she cooked, and Chris got the hint that she wanted to be left alone.

It wasn't that peculiar that she occasionally had a mood. They have had their difficulties in the decade that they'd known each other, but they were in a good place now. A happy place. Leah was the light of his life. Without her, he never would have made it through his computer science degree. He never would have survived his father's funeral or the financial struggles they found themselves in throughout college.

She was his steady rock, but he was aware that sometimes people needed a break from each other. Though they had hardly spent much time together since she started her new job at the five-star restaurant downtown, Chris understood why she might need some alone time. He'd never worked in a restaurant before, but he could imagine the stress.

"Alright, I'm just going to head upstairs and change," he said, giving her a sidelong glance as he made his way to the stairs.

He saw her whip around to look at him for the first time since she went into the kitchen. Her eyes were wide, and her lips were pressed in a tight line. She said nothing, but he was not blind to the worry on her face.

The dread sluicing through his stomach began to boil over. He thought he might vomit when he heard a thudding noise coming from the bedroom. Panic seized his chest. He rushed into the bedroom, just in time to see a nude man leaping from the second story window.

Chris ran to the windowsill and watched the man scurry across the grass.

"Hey!" he called after the man, but it was too late. Chris watched him scamper to a car parked a few houses down.

Trembling with fury and disbelief, Chris stumbled his way back to the kitchen. Leah was standing at the stove, her head down over the pot she was simmering.

"Leah," he snapped. "Who was that upstairs?"

When she turned to face him, there were already tears streaming down her face. He saw the quiver of her lower lip, and he moved around the table to look into her eyes. He needed to see her clearly when he demanded the truth from her.

"I'm sorry, Chris," she whispered.

She fiddled with the engagement ring on her fingers, twisting it up and down her knuckle. His gaze was drawn to the meager diamond he had saved up for so long to afford for her, the best symbol of his love that he had to offer.

"You're cheating on me," he said in disbelief, feeling his eyes growing hot.

"Chris, you know things have been rocky between us for a while," she said with a trembling voice. Somewhere beneath her quivering girlishness, he sensed her frustration.

"They have?" he asked dryly. "I wasn't aware."

"Please," she begged. "We never see each other anymore, and… I don't know. I just feel like we've both changed so much. I know I'm not the girl I was when I was fourteen. My world had always been so small, and when I'm with—"

She cut herself off and averted her gaze. Her arms were crossed in a tight knot over her chest as she drew herself as small as she could against the stove.

"With who?" he asked. "Who was he? What's his name? I want to know."

Leah sniffled and reached behind her to turn off the stove. He gave her a moment to collect herself, seeing the trepidation evident on her face. But as she chewed her lower lip, he realized she had no intention of telling him.

"Do you love this guy, Leah?" he demanded, the hot prickling in his eyes starting to form tears that pooled beneath his lids without falling.

She wiped at the tears on her cheeks with her sleeve and then fixed him with a stern look that brooked no room for argument.

"I think we should break up," she finally said. "I'm so sorry to have hurt you, Chris. I *do* care about you, I really do. I just want to experience more of what's out there. We're still so young, and I just don't think I'm ready for marriage."

Chris blinked at her, the realization still sinking in.

"You're the love of my life, Leah," he said. "I want to make this work. That other guy? We can forget about that. Let's not throw our relationship away because of one mistake."

"It wasn't a mistake."

Chris recoiled as if he'd been bitten. An unearthly silence settled over the kitchen. The pot on the stove was spewing up its last simmering bubbles. It was so quiet that Chris could hear the tick of his wristwatch and the low rattle of Leah's breathing.

"Not a mistake to cheat on me?" he asked, finally breaking the tense silence.

Leah shook her head, her brown eyes glimmering with a fresh wave of tears.

"That's not what I meant," she explained with a watery voice. "It was wrong of me. I know that, but I don't think breaking up with you is a mistake. I really think this is for the best."

Chris swallowed the lump in his throat and sucked in a deep breath for composure. Their lives were so deeply intertwined that he couldn't even entertain the idea of a breakup.

"You're not thinking straight, Leah," he said. "Let's sleep on it. We can discuss this again in the morning when you've got a clear head."

"I've got a clear head now, Chris," she snapped. "Listen to what I'm telling you. This is over between us. I hate to hurt you like this, but it's really over."

She reached again for the engagement ring on her finger and twisted it over her knuckle. Chris shook his head while she stared at the ring in her open palm. He saw the hesitancy on her face, the window of opportunity.

"Do not give me the ring back, Leah," he commanded. "We can fix this."

With a sob, she pressed the ring into his hand. She closed her palms around his and leaned up to press a chaste kiss on his mouth. He felt the tremble of her lips against his and drew in a shaky breath. His breath felt tight in his chest, like he could not fill his lungs up with the right amount of air.

"I'm sorry, Chris."

2

For the next few agonizing days, Chris was a listless ghost drifting through his life. At work, he got his tasks done efficiently, with a glazed unfeeling kind of focus, like he was numb to the entire world around him. He had shed no tears since Leah left that evening with a single packed suitcase loaded into the sedan he had bought for her.

She came into the house when he was away. He knew this because her things gradually disappeared – the collection of makeup and jewelry on the dresser, the stack of trashy romance novels by the television, even the hamster wheel belonging to their shared pet who had died years ago was missing from its dusty corner in the garage.

The day that there were no vestiges of her left in the house, Chris came home from work to find her key sitting on the kitchen counter. For a while, he did not move it, refusing to cement the devastating breakup by relegating it to a spare key to be stuffed in the junk drawer. It just didn't seem right.

After a week, Chris was a hopeless mess. He had trouble finding the motivation to pull himself out of bed each morning and go to work. Even mundane tasks were difficult to manage.

In a moment of weakness, he brought out his laptop and pulled up Leah's social media profile. He almost at once regretted the decision when he saw that she had officially moved into another man's house. He recognized the ginger-haired man as the same one who had jumped from his bedroom window.

Bradley was the name tagged in the picture of him and Leah at the bowling alley with matching, corny collared shirts. Revolted, he slammed the laptop shut. He couldn't understand how she could so easily throw away everything they had built together, all for some guy named *Bradley*.

It didn't seem fair. He had always been the perfect boyfriend. He never forgot a birthday or anniversary, always noticed when she got her hair cut or bought a new lipstick. He had done everything right, so why had she left him anyway?

Though he struggled to see her perspective in things, it wasn't as though he never had a wandering eye. It's just that when he saw a beautiful woman, he thought of her as nothing more than that. She could never compare to Leah – no woman could.

But if she seemed to think that there could be something better out there for her, perhaps, there could be something better out there for *him* as well.

For the first time in a week, Chris busted out his beard-trimmer. He styled his dark curls with some sweet-smelling mousse and dabbed a little cologne on his neck. It had been a while since he had dressed up to go out, so when he stood in front of his closet of work suits, he was not sure how to present himself for nightlife.

Eventually, he settled on a simple white button-down and a pair of slacks and headed out into the night.

The weekend's bustling spirit was high on the crowded streets. Chris wove his way through the quaint downtown cobblestone sidewalk, looking for a relatively calm, uncrowded bar where he could sit and relax.

It would be nice to enjoy a cold beer and know that he was free to flirt with any beautiful woman he might meet.

He found an alehouse on a street corner and took a seat at the bar. The air inside was smokey and humid, filled with the thrumming low chords of an acoustic guitar being played on the small stage.

Chris ordered a beer and glanced around the bar as he sipped. There were a few people dancing by the stage, and half the tables were filled with bobbing patrons nursing at their fruity drinks. Chris scanned their faces, unsure of how to proceed.

He had been out of the dating game since he was four-teen. It was safe to say that his skills were a little rusty, that he had no clue how to pick up a woman.

Fortunately for Chris, he was blessed to be considered conventionally attractive, growing into his aristocratic features as he aged. Though he always appeared gaunt as a child, by the time he had graduated from college, his reputation for rejecting women across campus had given him the perhaps undeserved title of *ineligible bachelor*.

Leah had always been a bit of a heartbreaker as well, and Chris had been so proud of their status as a power couple back then.

Even looking at the crowd of women in the bar, he couldn't find a single one as beautiful as Leah. None of them radiated her charm or grace. There was something magnetic and alluring about Leah that no one else on Earth seemed to have.

Chris choked back the rest of his beer, hoping it would drown the urge he felt to cry. He may have never picked up a woman at a bar before, but he was pretty sure the best way to do it wasn't bursting into tears over his ex.

He regretted his decision to come here tonight. The results could easily have been predicted if he had just thought for one moment, not acted on raw, jealous instinct. He could not simply waltz into a bar and find a woman of equal caliber to Leah.

He knew the things he loved most about Leah were not things that he could gauge just from appearance. Though his eyes were drawn to the blondes in the room, particularly the ones with the same honey wheat shade as Leah's locks, he knew that the warmth and compassion and empathy he sought were not hiding beneath blonde hair or brown eyes.

They could be in any of these women, and all he had to do was choose one to make a move on. Just a simple introduction, a polite conversation. He could do that, couldn't he?

But his legs didn't want to obey his brain. They twitched and bounced, perched on the scaffold beneath the barstool. He flagged down the bartender and ordered another drink, hoping the alcohol would dilute his reserved nature.

Deep down, he already knew he wouldn't be leaving here

with a woman tonight. It wasn't in the cards for him. He didn't even want another woman if he was honest with himself. He just wanted to prove that he could move on as quickly as Leah apparently had.

But when he went home that night to fall asleep in the bed that they used to share, he knew that he wouldn't be getting over her any time soon. At least not while he's living in the house they were supposed to start their married life in.

All he could see when he looked around the quaint, two-story townhouse were the absent voids of Leah's things, the clean ring in the dust on the mantle where her favorite Tiffany lamp used to sit, the empty magnetic knife rack glinting above the kitchen sink.

There was no way he could get over Leah in this place. He needed more space, a continent or an ocean between them, a place untouched by her presence. He couldn't continue on like this with his emotions roiling, threatening to burble over and destroy him.

3

The next morning, he called out of work. He told them he'd be taking a week of his vacation days and booked a plane ride to Phuket. It was a somewhat impulsive choice to go to Thailand, but the fare was reasonably priced, and he knew that it was a beautiful place with stunning white beaches and glimmering lagoons, the perfect place to get away.

He found a hotel near the bustling markets, and when he

finally deboarded the plane and checked into his room, he felt his first sense of balance since the breakup.

The air in Thailand was humid, with the tang of salt drifting off the sea. The sun was just beginning to set as Chris ventured out into Phuket's famous night market. Despite his jetlag, he felt a burst of energy and adventure as he strolled through the colorful tents and brightly lit market stalls. The sweet scent of baked pastries lingered in the air, and the advertising call of vendors rang from every corner of the street.

Chris wandered along with no rhyme or reason, stopping at boiled candy carts and sea glass trinket stalls. He had a mouthful of lemon candy when he heard the persistent shouts of an old woman to his right.

He glanced over and found her beckoning to him, her eyes wild. At first, he was confused, did not understand that she was gesturing to *him*. He looked around and realized that he was the one she was speaking to.

"Yes, you," she croaked with a thick accent. "Come to me. I have something for you."

"Something for me?" he asked, bewildered as he took a step closer.

She was standing behind a stall of glittering trinkets, with some ornate amulets hanging from long chains and jeweled bangles stacked in tidy columns. She moved beneath the counter of her stall, and when she stood again, she was holding a rather ordinary-looking wooden box.

"I sense it in your spirit," she said vaguely, waving her arm to beckon him even closer.

Chris obliged and stepped close enough to peer inside the box as she tilted the lid open.

"My spirit?" he asked.

The woman glanced up at him with her wizened, wrinkled eyes. She reached ominously into the box, and beneath the folds of white silk that cradled the tiny glass stone object, she pulled it from its depths.

"Your spirit," she confirmed. "Your loneliness. It's so intense I could feel it the moment you stepped into the market."

"Really?" Chris asked dryly, staring at the small, heart-shaped stone in her palm.

"This wasn't an ordinary shop, boy," she replied. "I know you're American, so I'll forgive your lack of manners. All the items in my shop have a fate, a set owner. I'm just the purveyor of the message."

He gave her a skeptical glance. "And what message would that be?"

"It's different for every person," she said, returning his dubious look with one of her own. "For you, this heart stone was fated. I heard it calling for you. With this heart stone in your pocket, your troubles with loneliness will be over. You will have much luck in love."

Chris did not believe the tall tale. He reached to pluck the stone from her palm and twisted it around with his fingers, checking every angle to see if it was truly something out of the ordinary. It appeared nothing more than a carved piece of glass, but he had to admit that it had a satisfying weight in the palm of his hand.

"I'm sorry," he said to her. "I think I'm going to have to pass."

He tried to press the stone back into her hand, but she stepped away from him and refused to accept it. She shook her head vigorously, throwing her hands up into the air.

"You must take it," she said. "You must. It calls to you. It wanted *you*. Do you understand? There will be other forces to reckon with if you do not accept your fate."

Chris blinked at her. "Other forces?"

"Strong forces," she said emphatically. "To appease them, you must buy the heart stone and keep it on your person."

He gave her a roving glance, wondering how many tourists this woman had tricked into buying her useless tchotchkes.

"I must buy it?" he asked in challenge.

She nodded. Chris tossed the stone into the air and caught it, testing its weight in his palm. The woman's face pulled into a peach-pit wince, and he realized that even if it wasn't true, she did believe what she was saying with some degree of conviction.

"Fine," he said, pulling out his wallet and handing her a stack of bills. As he was counting the money, he took pity on the elderly women and added a few extra bills to the stack he passed over to her.

"Remember to keep it in your pocket," she urged as she stuffed the money into a drawer under the counter. "It won't work unless you keep it in your pocket."

Chris slipped his wallet back into his pocket, eyeing her one more time.

"How exactly is it supposed to work?" he asked.

She gave him a grim, harrowing smile. "You'll see."

4

Chris slept well that night. If he had any dreams, he could not remember them, and when he woke in his hotel room, he felt refreshed and ready to take on Thailand.

The first order of business on his itinerary was a solo kayak through the Phang Nga Bay. He had always wanted to kayak or go white-water rafting, but when he had planned trips with Leah, she always resisted his more athletic and outdoorsy suggestions, much to his chagrin. She was more than happy to indulge him in some things, but kayaking had never been one of them.

Now, he had the chance to do all the things he could never do with Leah. He could hardly imagine her willingly kayaking into Phuket's dark sea caves, but just the idea of it sent a thrill of anticipation down his spine.

Before he left his hotel room, Chris glanced at the heart stone he had left on the bathroom counter. It sat beside the soap dispenser, ordinary and unremarkable. He didn't think it was capable of anything mystical or otherworldly, but like a totem or a palm stone, he found comfort in squeezing it in his fist.

So, he tucked it into his pocket before he made his way down to the pier and rented a kayak to take out onto the water.

With a map of the caves in one pocket and the heart stone in the other, Chris took his paddles and shoved out into the sea. The waves were gentle, lapping with tender ebbs at the white shore. The sky above was cloudless and blue, nearly too blinding to look at.

Despite the amount of tourists he saw at the crowded pier, the water was calm and quiet as he pulled out his map and set course for the first entrance into the caves. He was warned that they could be labyrinthian, and that he needed to pay close attention to his map or get hopelessly lost.

The first towering structure of rock pierced the sky in the distance, stark against the bright sunlight. Chris floated through its shadow, letting the cool air wash over him as he neared the mouth of the cave.

Mangroves lined the cavern's entrance, their roots spiraling in and out of the water in complex twists and whirls. Chris was careful to keep his paddle clear of them as he rowed through the narrow canal and into the chilly cave.

He repressed a shiver as the darkness slowly enveloped

him. He could still see the blue glow of the water beneath the kayak and a pinprick of light in the distance that marked the cave's exit. As his vision adjusted, the mossy walls of the cavern come into focus.

There was something ethereal about the place, like a sensory deprivation tank where he was somehow even more acutely aware of all his pain. There was nothing else to feel in here but the dank chill in the air, and Chris felt the sudden urge to lean over the side of the kayak and vomit into the sea.

He managed to keep his breakfast down and his paddles steady. The water was smooth beneath the wide blade of his paddle, and he focused on the physical sensation of driving the kayak forward rather than the jumbled thoughts tumbling through his mind.

At some point while rowing along, the pinprick of light in the distance disappeared. Chris's vision grew darker and darker the further he slinked into the cave. When he glanced behind him, he saw nothing but a black void, an emptiness that threatened to swallow him whole.

Panic filled his throat, clenching his heart so that each pounding pump of blood through his veins expanded it against his aching ribcage. His breath came in shallow pants. Without his sight, he couldn't navigate the caves, couldn't tell where he was going. His map was of little use to him here, and he felt growing dread burgeoning in his stomach.

Instinctively, he patted his pants, fumbling around for the heart stone. As silly as it was, he thought it might calm him down to hold it.

It was then that he noticed a faint glow emanating from his pocket. Startled, he fished into his pocket and removed the source of light.

The heart stone glowed in his palm, a bright, pulsing white light that crescendoed and mounted, cutting blinding rays into the darkness around him. He had to look away from it as his eyes began to sting and water. The stone was warm in his hands, almost hot. If he wasn't so afraid to lose it, he would have thrown it into the water.

As the light grew brighter and brighter, Chris felt it growing hotter and hotter in his hand, until he dropped it into the seat of his kayak. He squeezed his eyes shut, blinded by the intensity of the heart stone's light.

A mechanical whirring sound filled the air, shrill and piercing. Chris winced and buried his face in his hands. He didn't know what was happening, and the fear prickled at his skin, coating it with sharp goosebumps.

He could feel the heat of the heart stone in his lap, and he sensed that the light was dwindling. When the pinkness of his eyelids returned to black, he blinked his eyes open and stared into his lap. The heart stone was still there, its glow faded but still present.

But now, there was another glow in the cave, something ghostlike and wispy, floating across the surface of the water. At first, Chris thought it was just a shapeless white blob, like a formless entity.

It skimmed the water a few feet away from the boat, and as it turned, Chris saw that it was a woman cloaked in gossamer white silk, standing on the water.

At first, he believed he was looking into the face of God. What other explanation was there for this strange woman, this ethereal glow in the dark cave? She was not a creature of this earth, and he could tell just by looking at her.

He wondered though, if God was supposed to have a face like Leah's. Surely, it could not be a coincidence that this angelic woman had the same rich chestnut eyes as Leah.

It was *not* Leah, though. There were differences that he could see even from this distance. Her brows were darker and straighter, her nose a little more sloped. She was no less beautiful than Leah, which was the first time Chris had thought that about someone since he was fourteen.

"Hello?" he called out to the apparition, his voice cracking.

The woman glided closer to him, her stature poised and elegant.

"Hello," she replied, her gaze falling on him for the first time. Her voice was silky smooth and crystal clear, like a chime ringing out through the silence.

"Who are you?" he asked, his knuckles white around the grip of the paddle."

5

She tilted her head at him. He watched the smooth tresses of her auburn hair glide over her shoulders. Her lips curled into a soft smile, one that was patient and kind.

"I am whoever you want me to be, Chris," she said. "You've released me from the heart stone. I must have fallen into your possession for a reason."

Chris blinked at her. He was sure now that he was dreaming.

"You know my name?" he asked her.

She nodded at him, gesturing towards the glowing stone in his lap.

"We are joined together now," she replied. "I am yours."

"Mine?" he asked incredulously. "I don't understand. I still don't know who you are or how you got here. You live in this stone?"

He plucked the stone up from where it sat between his legs and closed his fingers around it. He felt an energy coursing through it, something potent and powerful, though he couldn't quite describe the sensation. Nevertheless, it was something tangible, something beyond belief. He had never been a superstitious person, or the kind of man to subscribe to any supernatural notions. This, however, was undeniable. He had visual proof that there was something otherworldly about this simple piece of glass.

"My name is Serena," she said.

Chris did not know why he half-expected her to say her name was Leah. Something about her was undeniably Leah-like.

"Come here, Serena," he said, assessing the 'ownership' she claimed he had over her.

Obediently, the woman came closer, her lithe legs moving fluidly beneath the sheer silk of her gown. Ripples splayed beneath her footsteps, leaving glowing footprints in their wake on the surface of the water. Mesmerized, Chris watched with wide eyes as she neared the edge of the kayak and knelt down beside him.

Hesitantly, he reached towards her face, expecting that his fingers would move right through her. Instead, the tips of his fingers contacted the impossibly soft skin of her cheek. He felt a shock of electricity course through him at the touch and recoiled.

"Are you lost, Chris?" she asked.

He wasn't sure if she was talking in a metaphysical sense, but either way, his answer was the same. He nodded.

"Put me back into the heart stone," she said, "and I will guide you through the caves."

Chris gave her a dubious look. Part of him wondered if he had succumbed to the insanity of his loneliness. He could not help but feel like he would wake up at any moment. It almost sucked the sense of danger out of the situation, though his body still reacted with sweat and a pounding heart.

"How do I put you back into the stone?" he asked.

She put her hand beneath his where he cupped the stone and lifted it up so that he was holding it at chest level.

"I will touch the stone and go back inside," she explained to him, her eyes glimmering when they connected with his. The eye contact was more exhilarating than the feel of her skin against his. He felt it like an arrow to his heart.

As she moved to touch the stone, Chris pulled it out of arm's reach.

"How will I get you back out again?" he asked. "How could you guide me from inside the stone? I couldn't see anything in the darkness."

Serena smiled at him again, and the sight made butterflies flurry up in his stomach.

"To call for me, simply kiss the stone," she said. "I will be waiting for you."

She reached for the stone again, this time, too quickly for Chris to snatch it away. He was not yet ready for her to disappear. If it was all just a dream, he was not ready to wake up.

But when her fingers came into contact with the heart-shaped stone in his palm, the blinding light returned, spreading, expanding, consuming the darkness of the cave with vigor and frenzy. Chris knew light could not be *heard*, yet, it rattled in his teeth and applied tense pressure to his eardrums like he had been plunged deep underwater.

A cry teared from his throat, though he wasn't exactly sure what he was overcome with that made him shout in such a raw and visceral way. He buried his face in his hands, waiting for the worst of it to be over.

When he finally opened his eyes again, the woman was gone. The cave was cast in total darkness so that his eyes may well have been closed. After a beat, when nothing happened, Chris released a breath he hadn't realized he was holding in.

Surely, it was all an illusion, a figment of his imagination. The adventure of being in a new country, of suffering through a breakup, of all his culminating feelings that he couldn't control, must have skewed his mind, given him silly visions.

He shook his head to clear his mind, desperately confused. His hands were still trembling as he began to row through the dark water. He was only a few strokes into his blind journey when the light sprung back to the stone.

This time, instead of a warm, emanating glow, the stone shone a beam of targeted light out into the darkness, a single ray shining like a spotlight towards the murky water off in the distance.

With little choice, Chris rowed the kayak through the beam of light. The stone sat precariously on his knee like a little guiding star. As his kayak glided through the water, the light moved and waned, pointing out the best path for him to take.

It was not long before the pinprick of the cave's exit appeared in the distance. Chris picked up his pace, rowing quickly towards the light, feeling a weight lift off his shoulders as it got brighter and brighter.

Soon, he could see the leafy mangrove trees that lined the

exit, and the dappled rays of sunshine that peeked through the canopy into the calm water.

It was with rejuvenating relief that he finally pushed the kayak back out into the open water, away from the murky, mossy, entrapping walls of the caverns. The sun warmed the chill that had lodged a place in his bones, and his heart resumed a normal pace. His lungs felt less tight in his chest, the air so clean and refreshing in his chest.

Out in the direct sunlight, Chris glanced down at the stone sitting on his knee. It was unmarkable now, no glow coming from the porous stone. Instead, it appeared just as ordinary as it had when the old woman had feverishly pressed it into his hands.

He was now more certain than ever that the whole ordeal had been nothing more than a wild figment of his desperate imagination. Surely, that ghostly woman had just been his own mind trying to fight for his survival. It had been his *own* instinct guiding him out of the cave, and it was ridiculous to think otherwise.

Still, Chris could not help but feel a little shaken as he returned his rented kayak and headed back to his hotel for the evening. Though there were still a few hours of sunlight left, Chris didn't have it in him to enjoy any more activities for the day.

When he was back in his room, sitting on his hotel bed, Chris set the heart stone down beside him and stared. He could not decide whether it would bring him good luck or bad luck to keep it. He wasn't sure he even believed in luck and had half a mind to return it to the old woman.

But there was something comforting about having it on his person. Despite his lack of superstition, he clutched the stone in his clenched fist as he laid back against the pillow and drifted off into a deep, dreamless sleep.

6

The next morning when Chris woke, the stone was still cradled in his palm. It was hot, but not unnaturally so, just the residual heat from his body melted into the rock. He gave it a cursory squeeze, and then tossed it in a short arc up into the air so he could catch it again.

He had a few more adventures planned before he left Thailand, and on today's agenda, was an elephant ride through Phuket's famous animal sanctuary. Elephants had always been Leah's favorite animal. They had seen them at the zoo before, but Leah was much too afraid to ever attempt to ride on one.

There was nothing stopping him from riding one now, so Chris dressed in comfortable clothes for the heat and slipped the heart stone into his pocket before he made his way down to the street to hail a cab.

By the time he arrived at the animal sanctuary, the sun was high in the early afternoon sky, beaming fiercely down onto the sandy earth beneath him. He found the guide he had booked online amidst the crowd of tourists and was led into a small enclosure with a single elephant inside.

It was smaller than the elephants he remembered from the zoo back at home, but no less impressive up close. The scent of manure and cut grass was acrid in the air, more potent as he stepped towards the wrinkly, grey elephant.

His guide instructed him to pet just the trunk with a gentle, open palm. Hesitantly, Chris stepped forward and put his hand on the elephant's trunk and gave it a few tender strokes.

There was a magnetic, compelling quality to the elephant's wise, black eyes. It made Chris's chest swell with a feeling he couldn't quite describe, something open and child-like, receptive to the world in an unencumbered way.

The elephant's trunk extended outward, reaching for Chris's other hand, the one where he held a large carrot the guide had given him. Obligingly, Chris tossed the carrot up into the air for the elephant to catch with her massive trunk before pulling it into her mouth.

Delighted, Chris asked the guide if he could ride the elephant alone. He wanted to experience what it was like to be alone with this powerful creature, wandering through nature on its back.

The guide was hesitant at first, but when Chris spoke the universal language of money, he allowed Chris to climb up solo onto the elephant's saddle. Chris seated himself in the short-walled carriage that enclosed the saddle and took up the reigns.

It was harrowing to have such a massive and powerful animal between his legs. As she began to take her first slow, ambling steps, Chris felt a grin spread across his face. The noise of the tourism faded away as he trekked deeper into the sandy woods.

After his experience in the caves, he wasn't sure that it was the best idea for him to be going off alone again. He wondered if he was in the right mind for all these solo activities that Leah always thought were too dangerous.

Another part of him was thrilled by the danger of it, by the lack of expectations he had.

Already, his adventure had spawned more spontaneity than he had ever found himself prone to before. Even his relationship with Leah had been carefully planned out and assessed from afar. Chris always followed a set path, a track that guided him towards the life he always wanted.

Now that the illusion of a perfect life had been shattered, Chris focused inwardly, scrambling for a different way to guide his decisions.

He followed his gut in this moment, seeking reprieve from his loneliness, yet somehow enjoying it at the same time.

Despite his growing and evolving independence, he still found himself wanting to tell Leah of his personal discoveries, to share with her his adventures in the single life. He could imagine the look of horror on her face as he recounted his time in the sea caves to her, or the fact that he'd now ridden on an elephant.

There was still the physical loneliness that he felt, and he knew that the cure for that was not so simple. He missed the touch of his fiancé, not even the sexual nature of their relationship, but the fact that he could hold her at night as he was falling asleep. He had not held a woman other than Leah before, and he could not imagine doing so.

Serena most certainly did not count, since by any account, she was not real. If he chose to indulge in his *owner-ship* of her, surely, Leah could take no issue with that. Maybe one day, she would see the truth and realize that Bradley didn't compare to him. Chris would have been the best husband to her, and maybe, he still could be one day.

But for now, all he had was the heart stone in his pocket. He pulled it out as the elephant slowly walked through a patch of shrubbery. He twiddled it in his hands, rubbing the pad of his thumb over the smoothed surface.

He knew it was silly, but he brought it up to his mouth and planted a kiss in the center of it.

For a brief moment, nothing happened, just as he had expected. But soon, that familiar, blinding light began outshining the sun, bursting through the air in radiant, crystalline beams. Chris winced, his chest tightening. He blinked, and when he opened his eyes again, Serena was sitting beside him on the wide saddle.

"Chris," she said in greeting, her voice warm and soft. She gazed at him with tender, affectionate eyes, the same look Leah had given him when he first brought up the idea of marriage to her.

The sight made a lump form in his throat. He still believed her to be nothing more than an apparition, but he enjoyed delighting himself in her beautiful face and angelic voice.

"We're on an elephant," she said observantly.

Chris grinned at her. "We are."

"Did you know that elephants are my favorite animal?" she asked.

It was in that moment that Chris officially decided that

she was a figment of his imagination, a sick replication in his mind of the perfect woman he had lost. She was the embodiment of Leah, a more ethereal version of her.

"I did know that," he lied. "That's why I brought us here."

"I've never ridden on an elephant before," she replied. "Aren't they dangerous?"

Chris reached for her hand and clasped her fingers around his. He was almost surprised to find that her body was, in fact, corporeal, a tangible, touchable entity. Her skin was warm and soft. He felt the pressure of her fingers against his as she returned the grasp.

"Don't worry," he told her. "You are perfectly safe here."

She gave him a knowing look, a demure glance beneath her lashes. "You kissed my heart stone," she said accusingly. "You must have missed me."

Chris felt heat come to his cheeks.

"I did miss you," he said. "Though I'm still not sure exactly what you are."

"*Who*," she corrected. "I am a person."

Chris quirked a brow at her. "Are you?" he demanded. "I don't know any people who live inside tiny stones. It really seems like you may be a product of my own imagination. How else could you materialize beside me like this?"

Serena shook her head ruefully at him, gripping his hand a little tighter.

"You don't understand the heart stone," she argued. "If I am not a person, then why did it feel like I was trapped in there?"

Chris didn't know what to say. It was a step of empathy he had not taken yet, to see her as a person with feelings rather than a ghost haunting his mind.

"I like it here, outside the stone," she continued. "I can feel the sun on my face and your hand around mine. It's nice. The heart stone was nothing like this."

"What *was* the heart stone like?" he pressed.

"Bleak," she replied. "It was a void, but a bright one. Like I was inside a machine."

Chris swallowed the lump in his throat, thumbing the heart stone in his hands, which apparently was this poor woman's home.

"A machine?" he asked. "What do you mean?"

She looked away from him, a tinge of pink cropping up over the bridge of her nose.

"It's like being plugged into a machine, docked in a state of stasis," she explained. "Like I am dormant and being recharged."

Chris gaped at her, unsure of what to think. When she explained things that way, it put her striking resemblance to Leah in an entirely different light. Who exactly was Serena? If she was not a figment of his imagination, then she must have been something else.

"You're a computer," he said accusingly. "An AI."

Serena nodded, dropping her gaze to her lap. "Can an AI also be a person?" she asked him, keeping her eyes hidden. "I feel like a person. At least, out here I do."

"If you feel like a person, then you are a person," Chris explained. There was not much more to being human than feeling emotion.

"People don't spend an eternity trapped inside a void," she ventured. "I didn't even realize how cold and dark it was in there until you brought me into the sea caves. And now here."

The steps of the elephant rocked and swayed the saddle. As she walked over a particularly uneven part of the ground, Chris clung to his seat for balance. Serena did not seem to mind, and only bounced slightly in her seat.

"That sounds awful," he said, his brows knit together in

concern. "How long were you in the stone before I found you?"

She gave a noncommittal shrug. "There was no concept of time in there. I can't say."

"Well, you don't *have* to go back inside," Chris said, confused as to why she never considered this before.

She peered at him with scrutiny, her brown eyes roving and unsure. "You won't make me?" she asked.

Chris gave her a look of bewilderment and shook his head.

"Of course not," he replied. "Who would do something so cruel? Do you think you need to do as I say?"

She gave another shrug, but her gaze was steadier on him now. She flicked it less often to her feet and allowed it to linger more freely on his face.

"You are my owner now."

Chris laughed at her, driving her gaze away from him again. He was amused by the hot red blush on her cheeks, endeared by her sudden shyness.

"Serena, people can't be owned," he explained. "Maybe you *weren't* a person, but you are now. I don't know how you came to be in the heart stone, but you can't be owned outside of it. You never have to go back in there."

She chanced a look back up to his face, her eyes wide and glimmering, reflecting the cotton candy clouds in the blue sky above.

"You mean that?" she asked. "Never?"

"Never," he assured her.

7

True to his word, Chris did not ask Serena to return to the heart stone, even when the elephant had completed her circuit, and they were ambling back into the animal sanctuary. He had no explanation planned for her mysterious appearance. He hoped to leave quickly after disembarking and get Serena to somewhere a little safer.

Her glow was less apparent in the afternoon sun, but

Chris still noticed when he squinted that there was something faintly radiant about her skin.

When they returned the elephant to its coral, the guide had a profound look of confusion on his face. He asked Chris who she was, but he brushed off the question. Flustered, he helped Serena down off the saddle, and she wrapped her arm around his as they made their way back to the entrance. He was just glad to know that others could see Serena too, that he wasn't just imagining her.

They easily slipped into the crowd of people. Serena let out a giggle of delight beside him that sent a skittering pleasure down his spine.

"Where are we going now?" she asked. He loved the sense of wonder he could see on her face, her sheer happiness that was obvious from the eye-crinkling way she smiled.

"Where do you want to go, Serena?" he asked.

She tapped her finger against her mouth, pondering. Chris watched with a smile on his face, captivated by every facet of her beauty, from her glimmering eyes to her pursed, pink lips.

"I think I'm hungry," she finally said.

"You think?"

She nodded.

"Then let's get something to eat."

They headed back to Phuket in a cab, crowded together in the back seat. Serena did not want to take her hands off him, as if he might disappear if she didn't touch him at all times. Her hip was always pressed against his, her arm looped tightly around his elbow. She leaned her head against his shoulder and released a sigh.

Unable to resist, Chris leaned down to sniff her hair. She smelled like fresh cloves of cinnamon and something faintly sweet and unidentifiable.

"Chris?" she asked him, her voice a hushed whisper.

"Yes, darling?" he replied.

"I'm feeling new things," she said. "Things I've never felt before. Can I describe them to you? I want to understand them."

"Yes, please do," he urged her. Her personhood was still somewhat in question, and he would take any chance he could get to understand her more.

She lifted a long, elegant finger and pointed through the window, where they could both see a line of acacia trees whizzing past.

"I feel like the tops of those trees," she said. "The way they sway in the wind, still tethered to the ground. How the sun mutes my skin… it makes me feel small. I felt so big in the heart stone, like *I* was the universe."

Chris rubbed soothingly at her arm.

"You are out here now," he said consolingly. "We're all small out here, compared to the universe. Now, you can know what it feels like to be small and unsteady like the rest of us."

"Will you be by my side while I learn how to feel all these new things?" she asked, tilting her face on his shoulder to look up at him.

"Of course, I will," he said, pressing a chaste kiss to her forehead.

For the rest of his stay in Thailand, Serena was persistently by Chris's side. It reminded him of how clingy Leah had been right after they left high school. He had gone to college, grown into his features, and she grew jealous as she stayed behind to go to culinary school. That distance between them during those years always bothered her, and during that time, she had always been physically affectionate with him in an almost desperate sort of way.

Serena was no less desperate now. Chris could tell that

she was quickly absorbing new experiences, letting them shape her new perceptions of the world.

He showed her what Phuket had to offer, taking her to try different kinds of cuisine, watching her graceful attempt at windsurfing. Despite her unwieldy emotional state, she seemed adept with the physical nature of the world: athletic, nimble, and lithe.

There was something inherently romantic about the whole venture, and Chris was worried that when he returned to America, Serena would disappear. It was almost like a fairy tale, watching Serena discover herself like this at the exotic beaches of Phuket. Would either of them be the same after they return home?

He pondered this when he booked an extra plane ticket for her.

It wasn't just that she'd be too perfect to exist. There were many other logistical questions to reckon with. This woman had no family, no identity beyond the heart stone he kept stored in his pocket at all times. She would need to get an ID, apply for insurance, and build herself a normal life in the human world from scratch.

By the time they finished sitting through the twenty-four-hour flight, Serena seemed very aware of how much of a burden her existence was. The airport was a scary place for her, evidenced by her saucer-round eyes and the clammy fist she kept wrapped tightly around his hand. She was beginning to see the common struggles of the average person, the hustling through busy crowds, waiting in long lines.

She was very flustered by the time they arrived at his house. He took note of her shivering as he urged her through the front door and into the dark living room.

"Are you cold?" he asked, reaching for the throw blanket Leah had left draped across the back of the couch. He wrapped it around her shoulders when she nodded.

"The air here is different than Thailand's," she said.

Chris smiled at her. "Yeah, it's much colder here. You'll get used to it."

"Will I get used to these other feelings?" she asked. "Sometimes I get this feeling in my stomach, like there are butterflies fluttering around in there. What does it mean?"

Chris canted his head to one side and stared at her curiously.

"Is it a pleasant feeling or an unpleasant one?" he asked.

Serena let out a hum as she thought of how to describe it.

"Both," she finally replied. "Or one or the other, rather. Sometimes it's very unpleasant, like when we were at the airport, and we kept having to rush around to where we were supposed to be. It was like I had a stomach full of bees, just gnawing away at my insides."

Chris let out a chuckle of amusement.

"And other times?" he pressed.

That agreeable flush returned to her cheeks, dusting across the bridge of her nose and even down her neck. He remembered how red Leah had been the first time he kissed her, how the redness had splayed all the way down to her chest.

"Other times, it's an entirely different sensation, yet, it still makes my insides feel like jelly," she explained. "It's like a warm, bubbling, sparkling feeling. It's wonderful, really. I wish I knew how to describe it better."

Chris tucked a single strand of hair away from her face.

"When do you feel like that?" he asked.

She averted her gaze, drawing her lower lip in between her pearly teeth.

"Every time I look at you," she answered.

The sensation she had just described to him suddenly invaded his senses. He could not help but smile at her, relieved to hear that she was developing stronger kinds of feelings. He could already feel himself falling in love with her, and it comforted him to know that she might be able to return the same feeling.

He framed her face with his hands and leaned down to kiss her on the lips. He could feel her pulse beating wildly beneath his palm, and he was sure his own heart was racing just as fast. She tasted sweet, like the lemon candies she had been eating on the plane. Her lips were soft and supple beneath his, and he felt a heated pleasure coiling in his gut.

"Chris," she said, breaking away from him by pushing lightly at his chest. "Are you sure I'm not too much of a burden on you? To open your home to me like this... I don't want to inconvenience you. I belong in the heart stone, you know."

A noise of disgust escaped from the back of his throat.

"You are *not* going back in the heart stone," he insisted. "I want you here with me. You aren't a burden at all. It would be my pleasure if you let me take care of you."

Serena grinned at him and threw her arms around his neck.

"Thank you, Chris," she murmured in his ear. "I feel like I'm becoming a real person because of you. I'm glad the heart stone found its way to you."

"Me too, Serena," he replied and leaned down for another kiss.

8

erena adapted easily to the world around her. Life as Chris knew it before the breakup returned relatively quickly. With Serena at his side, he felt lighter than air. Though he had been unaware of Leah's unhappiness with the relationship, there was no mistaking Serena's. She was truly delighted to be with him and fell easily into the role of his girlfriend.

It became entirely irrelevant to Chris that she was an AI. As she learned to develop her emotions and feelings, she became more and more like a person. Her flaws began to crop up, not marring her perfection but improving it. He liked her better with the stain of humanity on her, the ability to get frustrated and make mistakes. It humbled him...in a way.

Desperate to earn her keep in his home, Serena cooked and cleaned for him while he was away at work. His shirts were always neatly pressed, and though her cooking wasn't quite as delicious as Leah's was, it's always made with his tastes and preferences in mind.

He wondered sometimes if she still believed that he was her owner. The thought unsettled him, knowing what a responsibility he had to make sure not to abuse her fragile state. Her personhood always seemed up for debate, at least in her mind. She was constantly fretting over whether she was "human" enough.

Chris saw the humanity in her every day. She had an extraordinary empathy, that at first only seemed to extend to him. She was never unkind to anyone, but sometimes, it seemed like the Earth orbited around Chris, that she could think of nothing but him.

Yet, as he shared more of his life and the world with her, she began to notice the people around her more. She asked questions to the waiters at restaurants or the cashier at the grocery store. Chris could tell that her eagerness was off-putting to some people who found her questions personal and invasive. She never seemed to want to ask about the weather, but always about the last time a person had cried or if they have ever lost a loved one.

Eventually, the newness of life wore off for her, and neither of them had any doubts that she was a person. She could connect so easily to anybody she met now, like she had not just discovered all the different human conditions that could exist but absorbed them into herself. When others were happy, so was Serena.

It was the quality that Chris loved the most about her. He had loved that same quality in Leah, though not to this almost debilitating degree. He had to be careful with his emotions, especially those like anger or fear or sadness. She reflected them back as if they were her own, and in order to keep her happy, Chris learned to control his emotions better.

After a few months of living together in a perfect, warm, domestic bliss, Chris decided to propose to Serena. She was perfect in a way that even Leah was not, someone made to fit beside him and love him. He had no idea what luck would come to him on that flippant trip to Thailand, but he knew now that he did not want to live without her.

He was nervous the day he came home from work with an engagement ring in his pocket. The one that Leah had given back to him had been returned, and he used that money to buy another one, a simpler pearl engagement ring that he thought suited Serena well. Leah would never have been satisfied with anything other than a diamond, but Chris knew that Serena would be delighted with the pearl, that it would complement her elegance and grace more beautifully than a diamond ever could.

She was setting the table for dinner when he walked through the kitchen door. The smell of roasted chicken wafted through the air, and Serena had poured them each a glass of white wine. She beamed at him as he greeted her with a kiss on the cheek and sat down at the table.

"How was work today?" she asked him as she pulled the steaming pan of fish out of the oven. She set it down on top of the stove and fanned at it with her oven mitt.

Chris stared at her, enchanted by her graceful movements even when doing mundane things. He imagined her with his ring around her finger, swollen with his child in her belly. He could not wait to start a life with her, to make her his wife.

He had wanted to wait until after dinner so he could set the mood with candles and soft music while she went to freshen up, but he was too eager. He knew there were grander ways to propose to a woman, but there was something about the simplicity of this that spoke to him. To Chris, Serena *was* home, and to propose to her here symbolized how much he felt like she belonged here.

"Serena," he said, clearing his throat. She turned to face him as he wiped his clammy hands on his pants leg and reached into his pocket for the ring box.

She saw it immediately, her eyes locked onto where he held it in his trembling fingers. Her hands flew to cover her mouth, her eyes wide with shock. Nervously, Chris approached her and stooped down onto one knee.

"Serena, my love," he said, his voice quaking with emotion. "You mean the absolute world to me. The best day of my life was the day you rescued me from those caves. I have never been this happy with anyone before, and I didn't think that was possible. I can't live without you, Serena. I want you to be my wife. I want to spend the rest of my life with you."

A loud, rattling peal of thunder suddenly shook the windows. Chris and Serena both flicked their gazes to the splatter of rain against the glass. Their gazes drifted back to each other, both of them wearing sheepish smiles.

"I would love to be your wife, Chris," she said, pulling him back up to his feet so she could wrap her arms around him in an affectionate embrace.

He lifted her off her feet and kissed her, his chest swelling with a warm bubble of happiness. He was eager to begin the next chapter of his life with her, to put everything else behind him.

She pulled away from him to press feverish kisses all over his face, beaming from ear to ear whenever her lips were not pressed to his. Finally, he removed the ring from its velvet enclosure and placed it on her manicured finger. Serena held her pale, beautiful hand up to the light and wiggled her fingers, admiring the precious stone.

"A pearl," she cooed. "It's lovely, Chris."

She pulled him into another kiss, threading her fingers into the curls at the nape of his neck. Chris held her against him, his hands sliding to her waist. He felt the first stirrings of desire for her and deepened their kiss.

As his hands began to wander further, Serena latched her fingers around his wrists and gently pushed him away with a laugh.

"After dinner," she assured him with a final, chaste peck on the lips. "I worked hard on this halibut. Let's not let it get cold."

Chris gave a sheepish laugh of agreement and resumed his place at the kitchen table. His cheeks ached with the strain of the permanent smile adhered to his face. Serena bustled around the kitchen, fetching silverware and removing simmering vegetables from the stove. Chris watched her, his eyes drawn toward the ring on her finger and the sweet sway of her narrow hips.

They enjoyed her roasted halibut and drank wine, sharing in their happiness with one another. Chris didn't have a care in the world when he was with Serena. Laughter flowed through him in her presence, an eruption of the magnanimous joy he felt at every moment by her side.

Later that night, as they were slipping into bed, Chris removed the heart stone that had been burning a hole in his pocket all day. It seemed like a strange relic to keep sometimes, like a totem he hung onto with little reason. The longer Serena was out of it, the less it felt like the magical artifact that it was. He wondered what would happen to Serena if she separated from it permanently. He never really understood what she meant when she said she felt like she was docked to a machine inside the stone. *Did* it recharge her? Was the computer side of her fading as her human side took over?

The reality was that the heart stone was merely a piece of glass, at least, now it was. He set it down on the dresser and turned to look at Serena, who had already slipped beneath the covers of the bed.

"Do you think I should do something with the heart stone?" he asked her. It was the place of *her* origination, after all, so the choice should be hers.

"Like what?" she asked, flipping onto her side to face him as he slid into the spot beside her. She sank against his side, falling into his gravity, the dip he created in the mattress.

He let out a puff of air as he thought about his response.

"We should get rid of it, don't you think?" he asked. "I don't want you to accidentally touch it and get sucked back inside."

Serena shook her head, throwing one arm over his chest. She splayed her hand over his heart as if claiming it, the pearl on her finger glinting in the low lamplight.

"I couldn't bear to get rid of it," she said. "I feel like it's a part of me."

"You're right," Chris murmured in agreement. "Perhaps we should put it in a shadowbox and hang it over the mantle."

Serena was more approving of that idea.

"Perhaps," she said. "As long as no one else touches it. I'm afraid of what might happen if it were to fall into another person's hands. You've been kind enough to give me freedom, but others might abuse the power of the heart stone. I wouldn't want anything to come between us like that."

Chris hadn't considered that about the heart stone. The ownership aspect of things had always confused him. If another person kissed the stone while Serena was out of it, would she be forced to leave Chris? Or did she have to be inside the stone for the kiss to work? Perhaps it *would* be best to keep the stone in a safe place. If he was being honest with himself, he still wanted to keep it in his pocket.

"No, I wouldn't want that either," he said, dropping a kiss on top of her head.

9

A few weeks passed since Chris had proposed, and he was eager to set a date for the wedding. After his experience with Leah, he was uninterested in a long engagement. Unlike many of his peers from college who were already married, Chris wanted to be an avid participant in the wedding planning.

This worked out well in Serena's favor, who had never planned a social event in her life. She didn't even have family to invite, though over her short life with Chris in America so far, she had made many friends with her effervescent personality.

One night, after they had spent most of the evening choosing fabrics for the tables at the wedding, Chris took Serena downtown for a celebratory date. They took the cobblestone path from the house and cruised down the bustling streets.

Serena was childlike as they ambled down the path, pointing at flowers and weeds growing from the cracks between the cobblestone, and swaying her hips to music when they passed a loud bar. They arrived at the main square, and Serena pointed across the street.

"Look at that couple," she said with a sigh. "Don't they look sweet?"

"Not as sweet as us," he said teasingly as he glanced across the street at them.

His blood ran icy cold through his veins when he saw Leah's restaurant across the street. She was standing outside the entrance, her arms wrapped around the neck of the man Chris knew to be Bradley. He watched him kiss her on the lips and felt the first pang of jealousy that he'd felt in a while.

He'd mentioned Leah only in passing to Serena. She couldn't possibly understand how hard it was for him to see Leah like this, and he didn't want her to know.

Still, it was impossible for him to hide the look of agitation on his face, so when he felt Serena's hand land on his arm in concern, he dragged his gaze to her face and swallowed the lump in his throat.

"What's wrong?" she asked, peering up at him with her round, concerned eyes. "Are you alright? You look like you just saw a ghost."

Chris shook his head and placed his hand on the small of her back to resume leading her down the street.

"I'm okay," he insisted. "Just thinking of a memory."

"A bad one?" she pressed.

Chris nodded. "Kind of," he said. "Remembering it makes me sad."

Serena fell silent for a moment, lost in her thoughts. Chris glanced back over his shoulder to see that Leah and Bradley were gone.

"What did it feel like to be sad?" she asked.

Chris grimaced. It was one thing to help her understand the lovelier emotions a person could feel. To explain sadness and anger and fear was much harder. He wished she would never even think of those things and just be content to be happy all the time.

But he'd gotten to know her well over the last few months, and Chris knew how insatiably curious Serena could be.

"It's the opposite of happiness," he explained. "Sorrow. Dread. Like pain in your heart, but not your real heart. Like your soul."

"My soul?"

He nodded again. "It's a terrible feeling, Serena," he explained. "I hope you never have to experience anything like it."

Serena's footsteps faltered. She cocked her head to the side and looked at him with a furrowed brow, her lips pursed together.

"I think I *have* felt what it's like to be sad," she confessed, twisting her fingers together nervously. "Is that what it means to be human? To have a soul? Oh, Chris, do you think I have a soul?"

Chris frowned at her. "When were you sad?" he demanded, though not harshly.

"I felt it for the first time when I saw a squirrel get run over by a car last week," she told him, "and again when I went to make you your favorite dinner, but we were out of milk for the gravy."

Chris gave her a perplexed look and hoped that was the extent of any sadness she ever felt. He couldn't know what it was like for emotions to be so new, and he wanted to laugh at her, but he knew it would provoke more questions.

"Come on, darling," he said, pulling her into a strong hug and kissing the top of her head. "Let's forget about being sad for now."

10

Over the next few days, Serena seemed to lose the cheerful smile she always wore. There was something behind her eyes that was undeniably human, a look Chris couldn't remember seeing there ever before.

He knew exactly what it was. Sadness. The real kind. Serena was not as good at hiding it as most people were. He was dying to know *why* she had developed this new emotion, and what had brought it about. Yet, he couldn't bring himself to ask her. There was something traumatic about seeing that expression on her face, the very same one Leah had worn when she gave him the ring back.

So, Chris did the logical thing and ignored it. Instead of addressing it directly, he bought her flowers on the way home from work and massaged her feet at night before they fell asleep. He was quick to assure her that he loved her, to shower her with praise and affection, trying to bring those happy feelings bubbling back up to the surface.

Sometimes it seemed to be working, but Chris still felt something gnawing away at the bond he had forged between them. He had an overwhelming desire to shield her from everything in the world but him, anything that would program her against him. With nauseating shame, he briefly contemplated putting her back into the heart stone and letting her "recharge," as she had put it.

He didn't want Serena to slip away the same way Leah had.

One day, Chris came home from work to find Serena crying. He had never seen her cry before, and the sight of her with glassy eyes and a heaving chest hit him like a bolt of lightning.

"Serena, darling, what's the matter?" he asked, rushing to her side.

She shrugged away from his touch, much to his dismay. She wrapped her arms around herself, folding herself as small as she could make herself be.

"I'm sad, Chris," she said through her thick tears. "It made my eyes wet and my soul hurt. My soul *really* hurts."

"What happened?" he breathed, not sure that he wanted to know the answer.

"I've been out of the heart stone for a long time now," she said. "It used to stop me from feeling all these things. Sometimes I would get an inkling of a feeling, but when I went back into the stone, it was erased like it never happened."

Chris took a shaky breath and pulled her over to the sofa. With tender hands, he sat her down, rubbing the tears on her cheeks away with his thumb.

"It's overwhelming, I'm sure," he said patiently. "You'll get used to these feelings, love. No one said it was easy to be human."

She let out a watery laugh. "Did you know that there's a man at the grocery store with one arm?" she asked. "He told me he lost it in Iraq. And there's a woman I met at the library who is in love with *two* men. She's pregnant and doesn't know which one is the father."

Chris knit his brows together, unsure of what to say.

"On Wednesdays, at the farmers market, a group of actors get together to perform Shakespeare's plays," she continued. "The emotions I see on their faces are so real. It's hard to imagine that they are faking them. I don't think I can do that. How can I pretend to feel a way I've never felt before?"

The blood in Chris's veins grew ice cold as her words began to swim in his head. He couldn't really understand her point. He only knew that her raw tears were brewing up a sense of dread in his stomach.

"You make me happy, Chris, but there are so many other things I want to feel."

Chris instinctively shook his head. He licked his dry lips and sucked in a deep breath for patience.

"You'll feel it all in time, Serena," he said. "You can't rush the human experience."

"Part of the human experience is being able to make my own choices," she argued. "I love you, Chris, but you are still the owner of the heart stone. I can't truly be free when I am with you."

Chris glared at her, appalled that she would even think such a thing.

"You *are* free," he insisted. "I would *never* make you go back in there. You know that."

"I know," she agreed. "That's why I know you'll let me go back to Thailand. Alone."

Chris blinked at her, too afraid his tongue wouldn't work if he tried to speak.

"You gave me my personhood, Chris," she continued, wiping at her tears with the back of her hand. "I'll always be grateful for that. But I'll always wonder if you're still my owner, if what I feel is actually *real*. I want to know for sure. I want to feel things with other people and explore the world. I don't think I'm ready to settle down with you. There's still so much I have left to experience."

Chris's chest felt so tight he thought he might have stopped breathing. His blood was roaring in his ears, his fingers quaking at his side. He yearned to reach out and touch her cheek, to pull her against him and pretend she'd said nothing at all.

But the tears on her face were unmistakable, and her pain was obvious. It made him sick to see it, and even sicker to know that he had been the one holding her back.

"I'll take you to Thailand," he finally replied. "You don't have to go alone. We can explore together, just you and me."

Serena shook her head.

"You should have kept me in the heart stone, Chris," she said with regret. "This would have never happened."

Now, it was Chris's turn to shake his head.

"No, Serena," he said sincerely. "I'm glad I've kept you out of the heart stone. You *are* a real person, and nothing can change that now."

She blinked up at him, tears still clinging to her lashes.

"So, does that mean I'm really free?" she asked.

Chris stood frozen, his mouth suddenly very dry. Serena was waiting for his reply with wavering eyes, the engagement ring still tucked in her clenched fist. He did not want to let her go, and yet, he knew he could not force her to stay.

"You were never my prisoner, Serena."

She nodded solemnly and sniffled. Her hand came up to his, and he felt her press the ring into his palm.

"Thank you," she said earnestly. "I see that this hurts you, and that makes me so much sadder. But beneath that, I'm really happy that I met you and got to know you. You've done more for me than you could possibly imagine."

"I wish I did enough to make you stay," he murmured.

A quiet sob escaped her. Chris knew her emotions were still raw and overwhelming, so he wrapped her in his arms and held her tightly against him, probably for the very last time. He was sure she could hear his heart pounding in his chest.

"You should take the heart stone with you," he murmured as she sobbed into his chest. "I'll wrap it up well for you so you don't accidentally touch it."

"No," she said sharply, even through her tears. She pulled back just far enough to look at him, gripping his arms with trembling fingers. "I want you to keep it. You're the only person I trust to have it."

Chris's heart twisted in his chest. If she trusted him so much, then why was that not enough? He was not enough for Leah, and as it turned out, not enough for Serena either. He could not figure out what he was doing wrong, and he felt the pain of his failure.

"Keep it, and remember me," she insisted.

Chris wasn't sure he wanted to remember her after this.

"I'll never forget you, Chris," she told him, and she leaned up to give him one last goodbye kiss.

That night, after Serena had packed up what few belongings she had and fled out into the world, Chris sat alone in his bedroom. The room was dark, the blinds drawn. The ceiling fan overhead whirred rhythmically in the darkness, a thrumming, persistent reminder of his loneliness.

The heart stone was clutched in his fist, weighing heavily against his chest where he held it. He had thought about walking down to the river and tossing the stone into the water, but right now, he couldn't let go of it.

By giving Serena her humanity, he had also given her the ability to break his heart. He couldn't be mad at her for choosing to exercise the freedom he had given her. It was his foolish mistake for falling in love with an AI, for making the same mistakes with her as he had with Leah.

As he reflected back on his time with both of them, he couldn't help but feel like his only real mistake had been being blind to their unhappiness. He found it hard to recognize his own sometimes, choosing to ignore it rather than addressing it. Perhaps, that was where it had all gone so wrong. He saw what *he* wanted to see.

Regardless of how they had broken his heart, Chris wished nothing but the best for both Leah and Serena. He wanted them to find fulfillment in life, to achieve everything they ever wanted.

None of that quelled the pain in his own heart though. He closed his eyes and slowly brought the heart stone up to his lips. The stone was smooth and warm where he kissed it, and he thought he felt a bright light swelling in the room.

But when he opened his eyes again, it was still dark, and he was still alone.

The End

GAME OF HEARTS

ENCHANTED WISHES COLLECTION

Game of HEARTS

ENCHANTED WISHES COLLECTION

VIOLA TEMPEST

1

R oman rushed through the toy aisle at the department store, searching doll after doll. It was the fourth store he had tried that day, on top of the three he'd already stopped at the day before. But still, as his eyes skimmed for that bright pink and baby blue package — for the Barbie that Sadie had so eagerly begged for — he came up empty.

He stopped as an empty row sat nestled between two other Barbies. He leaned down to look closer at the price tag.

Barbie: Queen of the Mermaids. $30.00.

Roman clenched his thick fingers into a tight fist. They were gone here, too. How?! Why? Why was this stupid mermaid Barbie the chosen one for this year's little girls? And why had his sweet little niece been among the thousands of others who wanted this plastic doll?

Roman huffed as he stomped back out of the store and made his way through the brisk February chill to his car. People all around him were joyous and cuddling as the holiday of love lingered only a week away. Girls giggled into their friends' shoulders over boys' pictures on their phones. Women had a mix of stress lines and frustrated frowns on their faces as they checked their phones every few minutes. Men rushed in and out of the store, raiding the candy aisle, the flower displays at the front, and yanking giant stuffed animals out of cardboard bins near the cash registers.

All of these people prepared for Valentine's Day, while Roman slammed his car door shut and sped in the direction of downtown, looking for a plastic doll for his niece's birthday. Which just so happened to be in two hours. And his front seat was still empty of bags. He had only one envelope, wrapped around a blue and purple card with a mermaid on the front. She smiled tauntingly at him as if she knew his stress. She knew he had failed to find the only gift he promised Sadie this year. She knew how terrible of an uncle he was. She knew everything of his shortcomings.

He flipped the card over and sped up.

He was going to be late to the party if he didn't hurry. Maybe if he could make one more stop at the department store in Evansville. It was only another twenty-five minutes away and then twenty-five back, plus fifteen more to get to his sister's. As long as there weren't any accidents on the highway and rush hour traffic wasn't bad, he'd be just in time.

He gripped the wheel tighter as the urbanized part of town thinned out, and the close houses and small shops along downtown Main Street started to form. Sweat beaded on his brow as he saw red and blue lights dance further down the road. People's brake lights flared in front of him as they all slowed to a stop.

"No, *no!* Come on!" Roman yelled. He leaned back and forth, trying to get a better look at the damage, but all he could see was the butt end of a busted up semi-truck alongside a police cruiser. "Okay, okay. It's fine. I'll just turn around and go up Route 45 instea—"

Roman tried backing up enough to turn around, but the person behind him was too close, and the person on their tail was even closer. He wasn't going anywhere. He slammed a fist onto the steering wheel, and with his blasted horn, a shrill chorus of horns mimicked him. Roman laid his head against the cold steering wheel. Not today. He couldn't do this today. He didn't have time!

He glanced at the clock on his dash — *5:35pm.* An hour and a half. Wonderful. Just wonderful. He'd never make it to Evansville and back now. He might not even make it out of downtown in time, with the rate things were going — forget the Barbie.

Roman peered out of his window, trying to get a better view. That's when he noticed the small shop nestled in the back of the busy street among two huge weeping willow trees. He squinted at the unlit sign in the dim light of the evening sun and just barely made out "Aunt May's Antique Shop" swirled in loopy cursive. Roman had been downtown hundreds of times before. He lived only ten minutes away on the other end of their small town. But this shop… he had never seen it before. Never even heard its name.

He didn't know what it was. Maybe the stress of the last two days. Maybe his dire need to get *something* for Sadie.

Maybe because of the hopeless situation he found himself sitting in. Whatever it was, he found himself turning his wheel in the direction of the shop and parking his truck out front.

A low, dim light burned from the inside, and he took this as his invitation to enter. The door creaked violently as he entered and squealed as he pushed it shut behind him. As he glanced around, he realized that the "antique" part of the shop's name was right. Everything was covered in a layer of dust. The furniture was stained and worn with the stories of people's past. The wooden table at the front of the shop had cracks lining its surface and rings from old cups. Rusted tools, dated patterned fabric, crinkling book spines, and colorful ceramic models lined shelf after shelf as he walked further into the room.

"Hello?" Roman called out. But only silence answered him.

He rounded a corner, entering into another room, and then another, until he found the back of the shop. He heard a cough, brittle and raspy like that of an old smoker. He made his way toward the sound in the next room, but it, too, was empty. He sighed as he went to retrace his steps, but his eyes caught onto something in the back corner of the last room. He peered closer into the dim light and found an old shoe-box, torn at the corners and faded with age, lying on top of a wooden table. It was open, and its contents were covered with a thin layer of tissue paper.

Roman didn't know why he felt compelled to that box. Why he felt the need to explore its contents. Why he was drawn so closely to this exact place at this exact time. But in that moment, he needed to know what was inside. He peeled back the crinkling layer of paper and unveiled —

A tiny teacup with a doll in it.

Her porcelain white face glowed in the last rays of

sunlight seeping in through the torn blinds over the window. Her blonde hair glimmered and curled around her gentle jaw. Her painted lips curled into a coy smile that didn't quite reach her large blue eyes. The rest of her body was petite, dressed in a faded blue dress with white lace details. She had white gloves to match, and a tiny handbag perched under one elbow.

Roman stared down at this doll and found that he couldn't take his eyes away. That smile — those eyes — they knew something about him. It felt like they could see right through him.

"Ahem." A throat crackled behind him, nearly making him jump out of his skin.

Roman eyed the wrinkled and hunched woman in the doorway, just as she, too, peered at him.

"Can I help you, young man?" She croaked, that thick smoker's drawl reminding him of the cough he'd heard before.

"Yes, uh. I'm sorry to intrude. I just made my way in and started admiring all your... antiques." Roman coughed nervously as he brushed his dusty hands on the bottom of his shirt.

The woman took a step closer and glanced behind him. Her lips curled into an almost toothless smile.

"Found the doll, eh?"

"What? Oh, uh, yes." Roman glanced over his shoulder at the porcelain beauty.

"A gift for your girl I suppose? Interesting choice for Valentine's though."

"No! No, um, I'm not... no."

The woman's brow raised in question. "You're single then."

Roman shuffled his feet. Why were they having this conversation? Didn't he need to be somewhere?

Sadie!

"Actually, I was looking for a gift for my niece. It's her birthday today, and I'm on my way to her party. She loves dolls, and I thought this might do. Don't you think? She's beautiful."

The woman nodded slowly. "She is. She is... one of a kind, that one. Her beauty is unparalleled, but don't let that trick you. She toys with every man"

Roman watched the woman as it was his turn to raise an eyebrow. What did she mean?

"Anyway, I'm sure you'll be fine. It *is* a gift, after all. Now, are you going to pay with cash or card?" The woman waved as she made her way through to the next room and back toward the front of the shop.

Roman eyed the doll one more time, the woman's strange words ringing in his head. His phone beeped, and he checked the time. *6:15pm*. Shit! How had it gotten so late? He grabbed the box and closed it tight before rushing out of the shop and racing to his sister's.

∾

SADIE LOVED THE DOLL. It wasn't Barbie — Queen of the Mermaids — as promised, but it was unique and beautiful, and Sadie couldn't stop smiling at her new toy. As soon as she unboxed the porcelain girl, she brushed back her hair, straightened her clothes, and wiped down her fair face with a wet cloth to remove all the dust.

She named the doll Vivien. Sadie and Vivien hadn't separated once since Roman's arrival.

After a long evening of dinner — Sadie's favorite, spaghetti and meatballs — present opening, cake cutting, board game playing, and joking around, everyone outside the family eventually left. Now, it was only Roman, his younger sister, Olivia, and Sadie left. The three of them sat in the living room, Roman and Olivia on the sofa, sparingly watching some Hallmark romance movie on TV, while Sadie played with Vivien the doll on the carpet.

"Oh, John. It's always been you, hasn't it? You were my secret admirer all along."

John took Kate's hands in his own. "I was too afraid to reveal myself earlier. But now… I'm more afraid of not telling you and losing that chance forever. Kate — I want to spend the rest of my life with you."

Kate gasped.

The two characters on the screen then ogled at each other as snow fell around them in a light flurry. Olivia snorted as Roman feigned swooning at the confession.

"Marry me, Kate. And I will love you every day for the rest of my life."

"Yes!" Kate jumped with joy, and John scooped her up into a hug. The two kissed in the final minute of the movie, and the screen faded to black as the credits followed.

Olivia groaned. "I always hate these movies. They're so unrealistic."

"I think that's the point." Roman chuckled. "They always end with a happy ending. Everyone wants a happy ending."

"I guess."

"You don't?" He raised a brow at his sister.

Olivia leaned back onto the couch and sighed. "Of course, I do. It's just… not as satisfying knowing that those people started and will continue a relationship with almost no foundation built. They didn't go through hardship together or work to make a life together. They just found each other, fell in love at first sight, and then poof! Happy ever after. Real relationships take time, energy, and effort from both people."

"Yeah, you're right, I guess."

Olivia nudged him. "How's the dating front been for you lately? Any dates set for Valentine's Day?"

Roman laughed. "No luck so far. I can't even dream of falling in love and living a perfect little life with my Hallmark movie soulmate because I can't seem to meet anyone. Good or bad."

"It takes time. It'll happen when it happens. You can't rush love."

"Very soothing advice. Thank you."

Olivia chuckled as she pushed herself up from the couch. "Hey, chin up. Ms. Right will come along soon enough. You just have to be patient."

Roman nodded quietly, and Olivia seemed to take that as her cue to move on.

"Sadie, come on. Bed time."

Sadie groaned and asked for five more minutes, but Olivia remained stubborn. She told her to leave Vivien downstairs so she didn't get damaged in Sadie's "travesty of a room," as Olivia so lovingly referred to it. Roman gave Sadie a tight squeeze as the girl hugged him goodnight. She thanked him one more time for her present and ran up the stairs, all memory of her protest to stay awake and play suddenly gone.

Olivia told him she'd be back down in a bit, and she followed Sadie up the stairs. Roman sat silently in the living room as the next Hallmark movie started playing. He grabbed the remote and tried switching the channel, but it wouldn't cooperate. He sighed as he pressed the button again and again, but the TV didn't respond. Roman grunted as he pushed himself up and made his way to the TV. He felt for a button along its side, something that could change the blasted channel, but it was smooth.

"Can't stand seeing what you don't have?" A high-pitched voice squeaked from behind him.

Roman whipped around, but the room was empty. He swore he had just heard a voice, but no one was here. He turned to the TV again.

"I agree with you; those relationships are all abhorrently fake."

Roman turned as the voice, sweet like honey, continued on.

"You don't need something like that. You need something real. Something that will last." Roman looked down at the doll, who was now standing straight up on the carpet. She had a hip bumped to one side and an elbow perched there. She grinned at Roman's wide eyes. "What kind of woman are you into exactly, Roman?"

Roman nearly knocked the TV over when he scurried away from the animated doll. He crashed onto the carpet and crawled backwards as she stepped, one poised foot in front of the other. Her pink lips curled into a crooked smile as she stepped toward him.

"What? What are you?" he stuttered.

She laughed. "I'm Vivien. The doll you picked up from the antique shop. You know this."

"Yeah. But... but how?"

Vivien rolled her eyes. "It doesn't matter how. What matters is *why*, Roman. And *why* I'm here today with you, is because you chose me at the shop. You see, I'm chosen only when I'm needed. So, you, dear Roman, must have needed my services."

"Your... services?"

"Yes. And so close to Valentine's Day, too. How fitting." At Roman's silent stare, Vivien sighed. "I'm a matchmaker, silly. Men choose me, they tell me the traits they find desirable in a woman, and I give them an array of options to choose from. Sounds exciting, doesn't it?"

Roman hesitated at the light dancing in Vivien's glassy

eyes. Something… something wasn't quite right. But Vivien's warm smile put him at ease.

"Now tell me, Roman, what do you look for in a woman?"

"Um, well, I like women who are sweet, warm, and cute. Preferably someone who likes to read, like me. She could be an academic or not, doesn't really matter."

"What would your dream woman's career be?"

Roman scratched his chin. "Maybe a teacher or a librarian. Perhaps a nurse or a vet. Something where she could help and work with others."

Vivien nodded slowly like she was weighing his answer. "And her appearance?"

Roman smiled sheepishly. "I like blondes. Brunettes are alright, and red heads are eye-catching, too. But I suppose I prefer blondes the most. Blue or green eyes, fair skin, freckles, petite shape, just fit enough to be healthy without being overly muscular."

"And her social status… how does she interact with others?"

"What do you mean?"

"Is your dream woman very sociable, more of an extrovert? Or is she more quiet and subtle and introverted? What does her social life look like, and what does she like to do in her spare time?"

"Well, I think my ideal woman would be more extroverted than me, which wouldn't be too difficult," he chuckled, "but I don't see her being an extrovert all the time as that can be exhausting. Like I said, someone who reads in their spare time, enjoys small town explorations, dates at coffee shops and antique stores." He eyed Vivien, who ignored his pointed joke. "Someone who is quietly comfortable wherever she goes and isn't afraid to try new things, either."

Vivien stopped in front of Roman. She perched a hip out and rubbed her chin as she thought.

"You've given me much to think about, Roman, and I'm sure I will find you *exactly* the right woman by Valentine's Day."

"Yeah, okay."

Vivien turned on her heel just as footsteps echoed down the stairway. Roman glanced up at Olivia, just as she landed on the ground floor. She raised a brow at him.

"What are you doing on the floor?"

Roman looked toward Vivien, but she lied motionless on the carpet, just as Sadie had left her. Her lips curled into that coy smile. A chill shivered down Roman's spine.

"I, um, dropped something under the couch. Had to crawl down here to find it."

Olivia stared at him before shaking her head. "Alright, weirdo."

She picked Vivien up off the floor and set her on the coffee table. She asked Roman if he wanted another glass of wine as she stepped into the kitchen.

"No, I'll just have some water," he mumbled as Vivien winked at him.

2

Roman woke up the following morning, hungover by his dream of a talking doll. Olivia's husband, Carter, drove him home after the two additional glasses of wine his sister pressured him into — ones that he definitely… totally denied. He dragged himself out of his warm bed and groaned as the sunlight streaming through his window blinded him. He yanked the curtains shut before forcing himself to take a hot shower.

When he came out, he downed the two aspirins that he

had left on the nightstand beside his bed. But alongside the small pills, was a playing card. He turned it over in his hand to find the Two of Hearts. He sighed as he set the card down. Now he'd have to go through his decks and find where one card was missing. Great. The things he did while drunk. Roman dressed himself in fresh clothes. The headache wasn't gone, and it threatened to last for most of the day, but he was starting to feel better already.

At the chime of his doorbell downstairs, his gaze faltered. Who could that be on a Saturday afternoon? Surely, not Olivia. He knew she'd be even worse off this morning. Poor Carter had a handful.

Roman tutted down the steep steps of his townhouse before the doorbell chimed again, louder and grating on his ears. He grit his teeth.

"I'm coming!" he called out.

He stopped at the front door and jerked it open with a huff. Only to come face-to-face with a wide doe-eyed blonde. She gasped, her hand perched to ring the bell again. She hurriedly pulled it away.

"Good morning, sir. I'm sorry to have bothered you so early. But your mail… it was dropped off in my mailbox by accident."

She held out an envelope with his name written neatly across the front. Her long, thin fingers gripped the paper gently. Her nails were painted a soft pink. Her blue eyes peeked out from behind the bouncy blonde curtain of her hair. Roman took the letter, letting his fingers brush against hers. Her cheeks flushed as she looked away.

"Thanks for bringing it over. I appreciate it."

The woman nodded silently, but didn't move to turn away. Roman cleared his throat.

"So, um, are you new to the neighborhood? I've never seen you around here before."

The petite woman nodded slowly. "I just moved in two weeks ago. I live three doors down in 204."

"Ah, well, welcome." Roman smiled gently as anything more might scare the woman away. "I'm, um, I'm Roman."

She chuckled. "I saw… on the letter."

"Oh, right." He scratched the back of his neck.

"I'm Maeve."

"Maeve… is that short for anything?"

She shook her head. "Just Maeve."

Roman smiled, his cheeks aching from the infrequent use of those muscles. "Well, it's very nice to meet you, Just Maeve."

She giggled, her laugh as sweet and as gentle as the rest of her looked.

"Hey, I know we just met and all, but would you like to, um, go get a coffee with me? I have to confess, the place I've been going to is awful and overpriced, and being so new to the area, I don't really know where else to go."

Roman nearly stumbled at her abruptness. Even with all her shy, soft energy, she was forward and unafraid to ask for what she wanted. He liked that.

"Yeah, sure. I'm going to need some caffeine to soothe this hangover anyway. And I know just the place."

"Great! I'll grab my coat and bag, and come back in a minute then."

Maeve scurried back to her door, escaped inside, and within the next twenty minutes, the two of them had planted themselves at a local coffee shop. Maeve ordered a peppermint mocha with extra whipped cream, and Roman had to restrain himself from wiping away the whipped cream mustache on her upper lip. Roman guzzled down his usual cold brew as he watched this woman sigh with pleasure at the first real sip of her hot beverage.

"Oh, Roman. This," she pointed happily at the steaming

mug in her hand, "this is what I needed. Thank you for the recommendation. I never would have found this place on my own."

"I'm just happy to help. And I'm glad you're enjoying the drink." He smiled.

The two of them talked and laughed and joked for hours that day. Roman ordered and bought them gourmet sandwiches for lunch, and Maeve bought them a second round of decaf coffees afterward. Like her appearance, Maeve was warm, soft, easy to make laugh, and easier to make smile. She had many differing interests to Roman, like her love of kayaking and being outdoors — Roman was afraid of open water because of his inability to swim; her love of magazine reading and podcast listening — where Roman preferred to read literature; and her love of traveling and adventuring around the world — when Roman had grown up and stayed in the same small town his entire life.

They were very different people with very different interests. But Maeve... she fit his ideal physical attraction so well. And she was soft, gentle, and sweet. He enjoyed her presence, and he wanted more of it in the future.

He drove them back to the neighborhood that evening and dropped Maeve off at her front door.

"I had a great time today. Thank you for getting me out of the house and humoring me."

Maeve smiled. "Please, it was all my pleasure. Besides, it wasn't completely innocent."

Roman's smile fell. "What do you mean?"

Without warning, Maeve turned him around and pinned him back against her door. Roman's breath caught in his throat, and Maeve's whisper in his ear prickled his skin.

"I've been watching you for two weeks, Roman. You're so delightfully cute and awkward, and I wanted to talk to you much sooner, but I was scared."

Roman whispered. "Why?"

Maeve's smile curled into a crooked grin. She pushed her door open behind him, and Roman stumbled back into the dark. She then closed her door and locked it. And when she flicked the lights on, his eyes widened at what he saw. Pictures of him taped to the wall, scattered across the coffee table, littered on the counter. His breath caught. Maeve stepped forward.

"I've been waiting for this moment, and finally, it's happening." At Roman's wide gaze, she lowered her voice to a gentle whisper, the same tone that had reeled him in that morning. "Don't be afraid, Roman. I'll take good care of you, promise."

The lights flicked out, and Roman lost consciousness as Maeve's footsteps echoed.

He jolted up again in his bed, sweat beaded on his skin, but otherwise, unhurt and safe. The sun shone past his open curtains, and a raging headache rocked his skull. Two aspirins sat on his nightstand, along with a fresh set of clothes — the same set from before — and a playing card. But as he slowly turned the playing card over, expecting the Two of Hearts, he found the Ace of Spades instead.

3

Roman locked the door that morning to his bathroom as he showered. He peered over his shoulder as he moved around the house. He flinched at any noise outside, a particularly shrill car horn making his skin crawl and his head pound. He couldn't get the image of Maeve out of his head. Of the pictures of himself plastered on her walls and polluting her home. He thought they had such a good time. She was so sweet, so pleasant, and yet… she had turned out to be a complete psycho.

Should he call the police? But he wasn't hurt, and he *had* woken up in his own bed.

Roman cracked open his laptop and pulled up his work calendar, expecting to see his regular Sunday morning chat-in notes from the closers at his office from the night before. But the calendar was blank. He squinted at the screen. He always had tasks on Sunday morning, so where…?

He glanced at the current date — *Saturday*. What? No, but yesterday—

Roman clicked open his computer calendar, and it also read yesterday's date. He grabbed his phone, and the screen lit up with the same information. Today was… Saturday. Today was yesterday… but how…? Roman glanced at the card on his nightstand. The Ace of Spades sat idly on top of the wood. So dark, so solitary, and not at all the Two of Hearts. He sighed as he grabbed his coat and headed out. He needed some fresh air to clear his head.

As he stepped outside his door, he peered over to unit 204 where Maeve lived, but he paused. There was no petite blonde woman watching him from around the corner. Instead, a moving truck sat in front of the building, and a young family hauled boxes from it into the unit.

Roman watched silently until an older man, maybe the father, stepped outside 204 with empty arms. He caught Roman's eye and waved with a smile. Roman waved back hesitantly before getting into his truck. He sped off down the road, unsure of where he was heading, but he needed to get away. The traffic light ahead of him turned yellow, and he was close enough that he knew he would make it. But as he slid through the intersection just as the light changed to red, another car jumped out. Roman barely had time to gasp before the tire of his truck slammed into the hood of the sedan.

Tires screeched, horns wailed, and Roman's truck

skidded forward with the other smaller car in tow. When the screeching vehicles finally came to a halt, Roman gazed wide-eyed and hazily at the damage before him. He blinked once — twice — before he stumbled out of the truck and scrambled to the driver's side of the sedan.

"Hey!" he called out, his voice sounding foreign to his ears, "Hey! Are you okay?"

Roman hunched over and peeked inside the car, but the metal door crashed to the ground and out stepped a dark-haired beauty. A tight leather jacket hugged her wide shoulders, and black skinny jeans accentuated all the right curves. But Roman didn't even have time to appreciate the woman's dark silhouette and glowing brown eyes before her snarl cut him short.

"You hit me!" she shrieked.

Roman had to back up a step. "I… what? No, you hit *me!* I had the right of way through the intersection. The light was still yellow."

The woman rolled her bright eyes. "Which, if you didn't know, means to *slow down*. Not speed up, Einstein."

Roman bristled. "Hey, your front end came flying halfway into the intersection. You pulled up way too fast and way too far."

"If you weren't driving like a maniac and actually paid attention to your surroundings like you're supposed to, we wouldn't even be in this mess." She bit back.

Roman looked at the tall, menacing woman with a biting glare of his own.

"Look, I'm not going to stand here and argue with you. Just give me your insurance information, and I'll call the police. You're going to have to get towed."

The woman turned her vicious glare to the car instead. It softened ever so slightly. "I can't afford to get it towed."

Was this really his problem? He could just call the police

and let them handle the mess. But truthfully, his truck was fine other than some exterior scratches and a dent above his tire. It was her car that was lower to the ground and took the brunt of the damage. It was totaled, most likely. And even if she had pulled into the intersection too soon and too fast, he had also been flying through the light to make it in time.

Roman sighed. "Fine. Look, here is my insurance and contact information. I won't need anything done for my truck, but hopefully, they can work something out for you and your car. And if they need to call me, I can help as needed."

She sighed, taking the scrap of paper from his hand. She stared at it.

"Roman," she murmured.

He nodded. "What's your name?"

She tucked the paper into her pocket. For all her fierce confrontation upfront, she seemed unable to meet his eyes now.

"Hailey."

"Well, I wish we met under better circumstances," he replied lightly.

Hailey looked at him suspiciously. He noted the dark circles under her eyes that matched her dark makeup. All of Roman's fight dissipated.

"Hey, let me call a tow company. I have a buddy who works for them, and he can give us a discount."

Her eyes widened. "Really?"

He nodded. He called his friend, who said he'd be over in ten minutes. Roman hung up, feeling better about the woman and her poor car. He didn't want to contribute to her dark circles. He shivered as a cool gust of winter air blew past them.

"Wanna wait in my truck? The heat still works."

She looked over at his truck with the same suspicion. He chuckled and waved her forward.

"Come on, you'll freeze out here."

Hailey hesitated, but as another brisk wind fluttered through her dark hair, and goosebumps popped up on her face, she jumped into the passenger's seat. Roman turned the heat on full blast, watching Hailey's shivers turn to contented sighs.

"Better?"

She nodded. "The heat in my car doesn't work at all. So, this is… nice."

"It sounds like your car has some issues. More than just a crushed hood." He attempted a light joke, and thankfully, Hailey chuckled.

"Yeah, it's basically a trash heap. But it's all I have right now. It gets me to work and back, and that's what matters."

"What do you do?"

"I'm a mechanic and work primarily on motorcycles. But I also work at a homeless shelter during my free time."

Roman glanced at her. He could see the bike mechanic part from the way she dressed and her hard exterior, but a homeless shelter… that was unexpected.

"What do you do at the homeless shelter?"

"I organize meal times and contact sponsors to get donations for the shelter. Food, clothing, transportation, and experts in the community to come in and teach the people about things that will help them move forward in life."

"Like what?"

"Cooking, cleaning, job applications and interview skills, web applications, computer skills — whatever will help them prosper once they leave the shelter."

Roman stared in awe as Hailey warmed her fingers by one of the vents. This woman, so hard, dark, and fierce —

was strong, gentle, and supportive, too. He couldn't look away.

"What do you do?" She glanced up at him, her brown eyes sharp, watchful and warm.

"I'm just another office worker. I work at a publishing company downtown, just doing inventory and data stuff."

"Oh. At Goldfield's?"

"Yeah, you've heard of it?"

"Of course," she said. "I've lived here my entire life."

"You grew up in Alexandra?"

She nodded. "Born and raised. This community has helped raise me, and that's why I want to give back, however I can. Working at the shelter allows me to do that."

"Wow. That's… amazing." Roman smiled. Hailey stared at him and slowly, so slowly — her suspicion shifted into something warmer.

"Have you lived here long?"

"My whole life," Roman stated.

"Do you ever want to leave?"

Roman shook his head. "My whole family is here. My life. I love it here."

Hailey leaned back on the leather seat, the fabric squeaking underneath her weight. She sighed as she watched the moving cars go by.

"All my friends, extended family, dates… they all think I'm crazy for wanting to stay in Alexandra. They tell me that I'm young, with so many opportunities, but let me tell you," she crossed her arms over her chest, "people are nicer in small towns. People care about you and support you when you need help. And Alexandra — this community — has done nothing but help me. Why would I want to leave that?"

Roman smiled. "Exactly."

Hailey turned her gaze to him, and a slow, crooked smile of her own curled her dark lips. Something in

Roman's chest fluttered to life. But before he could utter another word, the tow truck pulled up in front of them. Both of them hopped out, braving the cold, as they greeted his friend, Travis. Travis quickly reeled her sedan onto the back of his truck, and Hailey asked him to take it to her workplace. She'd look at it when she could. She asked Travis how much it would cost her for the tow, but he waved her off.

"Nothing for a friend. I'm just glad I could help."

Roman thanked his friend, and Travis nodded with a smile as Hailey looked at him with watery eyes. She thanked him and watched as he turned away, her broken car in tow.

"So, what are your plans now?" Roman asked her.

She shrugged. "I guess my weekend will be spent fixing up my car."

"You think it can be fixed?"

"I just need it to run."

Roman nodded toward his truck. "Hop in then. I'll drive you."

She eagerly jumped back into the warmth of her cab, and he drove them both downtown, following her directions to the shop. Her car sat just outside a garage door, waiting to be taken care of. They both let a long exhale escape their lips as they caught sight of it. They then looked at each other after realizing what they both had done and laughed.

"I'm no good with cars, but can I offer any more help?" he asked.

Hailey raised a brow. "You want to help me?"

"If you'll let me."

Hailey smiled, the motion foreign and tight on her face, but beautiful nonetheless. She waved him after her, and the two of them pushed the broken car into the garage. Hailey assessed the damage while Roman watched. She pulled out a rolling toolbox with tools that Roman didn't recognize, and phrases and parts were called out that he had never heard of as she began working on her car.

Hours went by, and Roman helped as much as he could by handing her tools, offering her drinks when needed, and ordering food for them in the afternoon. This woman wasn't his ideal type in regards to physical features or her career choice, but she was wholesome, funny, energetic, and smart.

Hailey laughed at a poor joke that Roman made as the door opened at the back of the garage. An older man walked in, white hair and angry frown intact. He took one look at Hailey's car, and the frown on his cheeks deepened.

"What the hell did you do?" he yelled.

Hailey rolled her eyes. "I got hit, that's what. And I'm fine, thanks for asking."

The man tensed, every vein in his arms, every muscle in his neck, pulsing.

"I lent you that car so you could go to and from work, and look at what you've done."

"You *sold* me that trash heap of a car for work, and I used it without complaint, even though *I* had to put too many hours into it just to make sure that it worked in the first place."

"It worked, Hailey. That's all you needed."

"Yes, and it served me well. But it's life appears to have ended." She eyed the shriveled hood. "I got the rest of it working, but the engine won't stick. It's too banged up. And it isn't even worth putting a new one in at this point."

The man glanced over at Roman, perched on his stool.

"Who the hell are you?"

Roman paused. "Um, I'm Roman. Sorry to intrude. I, um, was just trying to help Hailey with her car after our little accide—"

"After I wrecked it this morning," Hailey cut him off. She

gave him a pointed look, and Roman tensed as the man did, too.

"So, it was *your* fault. You wrecked the car."

Hailey nodded slowly. "All me. Sorry, Dale."

Dale took a step toward her, and Roman leaned forward. But Dale was faster. He grabbed Hailey by the hair and yanked her face to within inches of his own. He whispered.

"I gave you this car, this job, this life — you little bitch. And this is how you repay me?"

Roman moved to help, but Hailey gritted her teeth.

"It was an accident. I would never go against you or disrespect your kindness to me on purpose, Dale. You know that."

Dale's lips curled into a snarl, but Hailey looked unfazed. The two stared at each other with cold, hard eyes for a moment longer before he shoved her away. Dale started for the door again.

"Get the engine to work, or you won't have a vehicle. I'll be back tomorrow."

The door slammed shut behind him, and Hailey let out a sigh of relief.

"Who was that?" Roman murmured, moving to her side.

She shook her head with a tight, sad smile on her lips. "Remember when I told you that this town had helped me when I needed it the most, and I wanted to repay the favor?"

Roman nodded.

"Well, Dale was one of the people who gave me a chance and set me on the path forward. He sold me this car for dirt cheap, gave me a job here, and helped get me a cheaper rent for my apartment downtown."

"But he treats you like dirt." Roman noted.

Hailey sat back on her stool and ran a hand through her thick, wavy hair.

"Yeah, well, whether my help was through kindness or threats — my favors have to be repaid. So, here I am."

Roman wanted to say more. He wanted to stick up for her when it seemed like no one else, including Hailey herself, wouldn't. But her somber smile and tired eyes made him pause. They really were two very different people, and he knew next to nothing about her life.

"Hey, you should probably get going. It's getting late, and I have a lot of work left to do here," she said flatly.

"Will you be okay on your own?" Roman eyed the door that Dale had exited through, but she waved him off.

"I'll be fine. Don't worry."

"Okay." Roman pulled out his phone anyway and handed it to her. She looked up at him in confusion. "Your number. I'll text you when I'm home, and I expect you to do the same."

She stared at him, her eyes and open mouth wide in shock. She slowly took his phone, and with shaky fingers, entered her number. He smiled when she handed it back.

"You be safe tonight, and don't stay up too late with this car, okay? If you need help or, more likely, moral support, I'm here."

Her lips cracked into a tight smile, and she nodded.

"Thanks. I appreciate it. Really."

With that, Roman hopped into his own truck outside and made his way back to the townhouse. He texted Hailey after locking the door behind him.

I'm home. :-)

Hailey responded back almost immediately. *Thanks for the company today. I appreciate all your help.*

Roman grinned at his phone before setting it on his nightstand. He watched two episodes of some comedy special on cable, and before he knew it, he nodded off.

When he woke up the next morning, he eagerly grabbed

his phone and scrolled through his messages, but nowhere in his history was there a Hailey. He eyed his nightstand in the light of the morning, and on its surface, sat two aspirins, a set of clothes, and a playing card.

Roman's breath hitched as he turned the card over. In the rays of light streaming past his curtains, he came face-to-face with the Queen of Diamonds.

4

Roman searched through his contacts, but Hailey's number was nowhere to be seen. He rushed outside after, glanced down at building 204, and found the mailbox decorated with children's handprints and a different last name than he remembered from Maeve's residence. It was like neither of them, Maeve or Hailey, even existed. Had he really met them? Were they real at all? He pulled out his phone and glanced at the screen — *Saturday*, it read.

What was happening? Why was he living Saturday over

and over again but differently? Meeting two different women and living two very different days. He must be losing it.

Roman grabbed his coat and moved toward the door, but his phone rang. He paused and stared at the unidentified number on his screen. It had his area code, and while he usually doesn't pick up phone calls from random numbers, something told him to answer this one.

"Hello?" he said, propping the phone to his ear.

A high-pitched woman's voice echoed through the line.

"Hello. Is this Mr. Roman Wright?"

"Yeah. Who's this?"

"Good morning, sir. Sorry to bother you, but we have your niece, Sadie, here at school. She appears to have a slight fever. We contacted her parents but, unfortunately, her father appears to be out of town, and her mother's phone went to voicemail. Your phone number was next in line on the emergency contact list."

"School? Why's she even in school on a Saturday?"

"Don't you know, sir? Sadie comes in with some other kids on Saturdays for extra tutoring. She's been doing so for months now."

"Oh." Roman threw on his coat, straining his arms through the sleeves as he tried not to drop his phone. "Do you need me to come get her then?"

"Yes, sir. She cannot stay at school with a fever. She needs time and rest to recuperate. I will try to call her mother again, but for now, you will need to come get her."

"Okay. That's fine. I can head out now. I'll be there in five minutes."

"Perfect. We will see you soon."

With that, Roman hung up and raced for his truck. The engine took three or four tries to turn over in the cold morning air, but once it rumbled to life, he floored it out of the parking lot. He made it to Sadie's elementary school in four minutes and rushed to the office. He quickly filled out the necessary paperwork for Sadie's release and then made his way to the nurse's office, where Sadie sat swinging her legs over the side of the nurse's examination bed.

"Uncle Roman!" she called as he smiled at her. He pulled her into a tight hug and stroked her hair.

"Hey, you. Not feeling well?"

She shook her head. "My head was hurting this morning, and Mommy gave me Tylenol, but it didn't work. My head still hurts. So, I came to the nurse, and she took my temperature, and now I have a fever."

"So, she'll need lots of water, rest, and maybe some cool rags for her head." Roman looked up at the honey sweet voice, only to find a red-headed woman perched in the doorway to the desk area of the school infirmary. She smiled at him before meeting Sadie's eyes. "Get some Gatorade on your way home, alright? The electrolytes will help. Once you're home, it's straight to bed and lots of rest, okay?"

Sadie nodded sharply. "Yes, Ms. Miller."

Ms. Miller smiled. "Good. Now, Mr. Wright, if you'll step into my office for a moment, I just need you to sign a few papers, and you two can be on your way."

Roman nodded and followed the woman into her office space. She closed the door behind her and pulled out the extra chair beside her desk.

"Have a seat." Once he sat down, she set three sheets of paper in front of him. "I need you to read and sign the bottom of each one. The first goes over the patient release information and acceptance; that one's for the school's records. The next is for the state, acknowledging that I examined and treated Sadie to the best of my abilities as her nurse. And the final one is for my records, just acknowledging Sadie's visit, her complaints, symptoms, and the resolution. Which, obviously, was to send her home with you."

"Okay." Roman signed each one after skimming their contents. Once he finished, she stacked the papers into a neat pile and set them on the center of her desk.

"Wonderful! Thank you for coming to get Sadie today. I tried her mom again, but she didn't answer. I hope she's alright."

"It *is* odd. I'll try her after I get Sadie home. But thank you for taking care of her, Ms. Miller."

"Oh, you can call me Brielle." She smiled easily. Her painted pink lips were peachy and smooth against her freckled skin and burning red hair.

"Well, thank you again, Brielle." Roman smiled, too.

They both moved for the door, but before Roman could push it open, it was yanked away from him from the opposite side. A sweaty and panting Olivia stood in the doorway.

"Sadie, is she okay?" She gasped before noticing Roman. "Romy? What are you doing here?"

"The nurse called me when she couldn't get a hold of you. I came to get Sadie."

Brielle stepped out from behind him and waved at Olivia.

"Hello, Mrs. Finkle. I apologize for the confusion and anxiety. Sadie is doing just fine. She just has a slight fever and needs to rest at home."

"Oh." Olivia turned as Sadie ran up to her side and gripped her forearm with a smile.

"Mommy, I'm ready to go home now."

Olivia glanced at the three of them and nodded slowly as the panic seemed to slip away. She patted Sadie's head. "Okay, sweetie. We're going." She waved at the two of them before grabbing Sadie's backpack and turning out of the infirmary.

Roman let out a short sigh. "Well, I guess she's got her then."

Brielle chuckled lightly. "You're off the hook."

"Guess so." He scratched the back of his neck.

"Do you have any children of your own here?"

"No," he said, "just Sadie, my niece."

"And yet, you came so quickly."

"Yeah. I mean, Sadie was sick and needed help. Why wouldn't I come quickly?"

Brielle chuckled as she settled back into the chair behind her desk. "You'd be surprised how many parents take their good ol' time when I call them, telling them their children are sick and need to be picked up. So, the fact that Sadie isn't even yours, and you still came very quickly — you must really care about her."

Roman nodded easily. "She's my niece, my only niece. She means the world to me, and I'd do anything for that kid."

Brielle smiled up at him. "That's good to know. I mean, if she ever falls ill again, and I can't contact her parents, of course."

"Of course." Roman chuckled.

"Hey, I know this may seem a bit out there and probably, totally, unprofessional, but are you free tonight?"

Roman paused in the doorway. Had he heard her right?

"You... you're asking me out?"

Brielle smirked, her white nurse's coat hanging around her shoulders and draping past the hemline of her skirt so perfectly that it looked like there might just be nothing underneath the white lab coat. Until she shifted, of course. She crossed her thick thighs and caused the skirt to rise a little higher on her skin as she turned to him.

"I probably shouldn't be, but yes, I am. I'm, um, going to a party with some friends at the bar tonight, and no matter how many times I've told them that I don't need a man at my side or a boyfriend, they pester me nonstop about my lack of a date. And while I was mentally preparing all morning to listen to those teasing remarks all night, you stepped in. Young, handsome, and caring. And honestly, what else could I ask for?"

Roman was speechless. This woman — curvy and beautiful and smart and sweet — wanted to go out with him. After only knowing him for twenty minutes. After only talking to him once. All because he loved Sadie and was worried for her health.

Roman glanced at the clock on the far wall. It was still early afternoon, and being that it was Saturday, yet again, he had nothing else to do. He shrugged.

"Why not? I'll be your date."

Brielle nearly squealed with delight. "Really? Wait, seriously?"

"Yeah." Roman chuckled nervously. "You *were* being serious, right?"

"Yes! Oh, yes. Completely! I just didn't think — oh! This is perfect! Thank you, Roman, or is it Romy?"

"Roman is just fine."

"Classy and original. I adore it." She actually squealed this time as she walked him to the door. "Okay, I will send you a message with the time and everything, and meet you there. Dress casual; it's just a bar, you know? Oh, thank you, thank you, Roman! I really appreciate it. Really, you can't even imagine the amount of pestering you've saved me from."

Roman chuckled. "It's no problem. I'll see you tonight."

"Yes! See you tonight!" Brielle turned on her heel back into the office, and Roman grinned as he heard her squeal in her office.

He made his way down the hall and out to his truck. His phone beeped as he started the engine. He glanced at it and found a text from a new number. It said they were meeting tonight at eight and thanked him *again* for coming. It was signed "Bri."

Roman smiled to himself as he drove home. He spent the rest of the afternoon cleaning his house, and then himself before the evening. By the time eight rolled around, he sat outside the bar in his truck, his hair damp from the shower and styled just perfectly messy, his jawline covered with a light shadow, and his body dressed in a button-down shirt with his favorite jeans that fit just right. But as he stepped inside the bar and glanced around for Brielle, he didn't find a buttoned-up nurse in a lab coat. Instead, a woman found his eyes from across the room. She smiled, the only thing similar to the woman he had spoken to that morning. The rest of her, however, made his jaw drop.

She wore a tight skirt that came up to her mid-thigh, with thigh-high socks that stretched up and squeezed, revealing that tiniest hint of skin on her legs. High boots hugged her calves and accentuated her long legs. And a sparkly belt around her pink lace top cinched her waist into a perfect hourglass shape. Her pink lips had shifted into a dark, almost blood red, shade, making her green eyes shimmer and her freckled skin glow. Her hair burned like fire under the rotating bar lights. They shifted red as she made her way over to him, and he saw nothing but a fierce being of fire and flame.

"Hey, I'm glad you made it," she called out once she was close enough for him to hear over the music and loud chatter.

Roman followed her to her group. "Wouldn't miss it. Like Sadie, I didn't want to leave you stranded."

She chuckled. "I appreciate that." She stopped at the edge of a round table surrounded by five other people. Three females and two males. They all looked at him with either skepticism or wonder. He swallowed down his uneasiness and forced a smile instead.

"This is Roman, my *date*," Brielle emphasized.

The girls' eyes widened with excitement while the guys looked at him.

"This is him? Wow, good choice, Bri. He *is* cute."

"Totally. Where'd you snatch him?" Two of the girls chimed.

Brielle smiled at him. "At work. He came to pick up his niece. He was so good with her; I couldn't take my eyes off him."

Roman nodded a little too quickly.

"Aw," one girl cooed, "a *daddy*."

Brielle gave her friend a light shove, and they all giggled. Roman wavered. He wasn't used to this social life — late nights at a bar, outings with big groups of friends, introductions, first impressions…

Roman always stayed within his circle. His tight little circle of family and friends. He enjoyed spending time with them regularly and attending the occasional party, but this? This was way out of his comfort zone. What was he even doing here? Why did he say yes? The lights spun too fast and too bright, the music beat too loudly, thumping through his limbs and vibrating his bones; the people surrounding him all reeked of pungent cologne and sweat, and this place was unapologetically stuffy. He preferred the cold February air outside over this.

Brielle laughed at something that one of her male friends had said. At her smile, Roman's panic curbed the slightest bit. He was there to support her. He told her he would, and he wouldn't back out now just because he felt outside his comfort zone.

"She's a beauty, isn't she?" A female voice echoed to his

left. He glanced up and found a pair of brown eyes on him. She was one of Brielle's friends.

Roman followed her gaze to Brielle. He smiled. "She is. Her laugh, her charm, her ease… it's contagious."

Her friend nodded, her smile warming. "Do you like her? I know she said you're her date for tonight, but we all figured she begged you to come last minute to avoid our teasing."

"You knew," he mumbled, but his smile only widened as Brielle looked up to lock eyes with him. Her red lips curled into a wide grin, and something in his chest tightened. "She's the complete opposite of me, but she's… well… I do like her."

Her friend made room as Brielle climbed onto the bench beside him. They all spent the night talking, laughing, gossiping about small town life. Roman admittedly felt anxious at first, but as the night came to a close, and Brielle gave him a peck on the cheek before driving off with her friends, he couldn't help but feel happy.

5

Roman woke up the following morning expecting sunshine through his window, the curtain pushed aside, and a headache behind his eyes. But when he opened his eyes, it was raining outside his window. He sat up and tilted his head, but the headache had disappeared, too.

He glanced down at his nightstand, expecting two aspirins, his clothes, and the standard playing card of the day. But none of those were there. His table sat empty except for his phone. He picked it up, and the screen flickered to life.

Sunday.

Something white sat on the nightstand underneath where his phone was. His eyes turned on it and found another playing card. He picked it up and turned it over slowly. It was the Joker.

A crash from the kitchen steeled his spine. Roman grabbed the bat that he kept in his closet and crept down the stairs. Each step creaked under his weight, and he flinched at the noise. But the crashes in the kitchen didn't stop. He rounded the last corner to the room and paused as he peeked in, and there, on the kitchen island, sat Vivien the doll on the napkin holder. She sipped from a tiny teacup, unbothered by his ensuing presence.

"What? How? What are you doing here?" He gaped as he threw down the bat.

She barely glanced up at him. "Good to see you again, Roman."

"Vivien… what?"

"I'm here for your decision, Roman."

"What are you talking about?"

"Don't play dumb. Surely, you've noticed the last three Saturdays you've gotten to enjoy with three very different women."

Roman thought back to the cards, the date on his phone, the identical setting each morning…

Vivien pulled three cards from the tabletop. She held them up one by one.

"The Two of Hearts. Sweet, quiet, and warm. Cute, right? Maeve fits your desired physical traits to the dot. But that obsessive personality, it's… interesting.

"The Ace of Spades. Dark, mysterious, independent. Hailey is a fiery one, and so wholesome, too. But the baggage she carries…" Vivien blew out a low whistle.

"And the Queen of Diamonds. Wild, strong, and hot. Brielle was almost the opposite of what you described in a woman, but she's also a nurse and loves children. She'd probably push you out of your comfort zone."

"They were all great, at first. Each of them had traits that I liked," Roman answered slowly.

Vivien nodded. "But...?"

"But they were also so different from my ideal. And so different from me. Maeve seemed perfect in all regards, but she turned out to be a bit... psychotic. Hailey *is* wholesome but carries too much on her shoulders. And Brielle loves kids and helps them like I wanted, but her social life is way out of my comfort zone."

"I see." Vivien looked at him, that coy grin still on her lips. "So, none of the women suited your ideal just right."

Roman wavered. He enjoyed his time with all the women and had come to like them. But he saw the issues that would emerge in the future if he were to pursue them. Maeve's obsession was a no-brainer, Hailey's baggage would catch up to her and maybe drag her down forever, and Brielle was too extroverted; she'd grow bored of Roman and look elsewhere for fulfillment.

"I just don't see any of the relationships working long-term."

"So, you choose none?"

Roman eyed the cards on the table and thought back on the last three days. But all he could see was the obsessiveness, the baggage, and the extroversion; none of these women were just right for him.

"I choose none... for now."

Vivien's smile cracked into a wide grin. "That's unfortunate. And I thought Hailey and Brielle had a solid chance. Oh, well."

"They were great. But the differences between us were too significant. Would you be able to summon another woman?"

Vivien pulled the last card from the tabletop and held it up to him. The Joker.

"No, Roman, I can't. Because this is the end of the line for you."

"What do you mean? I thought you were going to get me a perfect woman before Valentine's Day."

"I did. Three of them, in fact. Three of them who suited your needs in some way. But like any living person on this Earth, they didn't fit your ideal to the very last dot. Because human beings are all unique, all of them have strengths and weaknesses, and things that set them apart from everyone else. And you, Roman, *still* chose none of them."

"Wait, but I—"

"There's a deal with my game here. I give you three women, and you choose which one you'd like to keep in your lonely little life. If you choose, *boom*! She's yours. But if you see only the negatives, only the traits that the women *don't* have, and choose none of them, well," she tilted her porcelain little head at him, "then you get nothing."

"But you… but—"

Vivien slinked off the napkin holder and dropped the Joker onto the table, right on top of the other cards.

"Even when three amazing women were dropped at your feet, you still chose none of them." She shook her head. "You deserve to rot alone, Roman."

"Wait, Vivien, I—"

"Oh, well, off to my next adventure. Enjoy your pitiful, lonely life, Roman."

Before he could say another word to stop her, she vanished. Roman stared at the spot where she had been, the four cards staring up at him, accusing him, taunting him for his mistake. He left them there until the following Saturday, and then he threw them into the trash. For this Valentine's Day and all the ones following, he spent alone.

The End

DATING THE DAMSEL

ENCHANTED WISHES COLLECTION

Dating the DAMSEL

ENCHANTED WISHES COLLECTION

VIOLA TEMPEST

Scarlett ran through the front door, tears streaming down her face, before throwing herself onto the couch. I jumped at her entrance, but at the sight and sound of the sobs racking through her small body, my muscles relaxed. I let out a slow sigh before getting up, nudging the front door closed, and making my way over to her trembling form, curled on the couch cushions.

I nudged her hand with my wet nose until it rested across

my neck. I let out a low grumble, trying to get her to look at me. *Scarlett*, I grumbled, *look at me, please.* At times like this, I wish more than anything that I could soothe her with words that she would understand.

Sobs racked Scarlett's small frame. Her thin shoulders shook as short gasps clawed out from her throat. The congestion in her throat and her nose were audible. She had been crying for some time. That thought made my chest tighten and squeeze even more. I nudged her hair away from her downturned face, sniffling in her ear. She normally swatted me away for blowing air into her ears, her smile full of laughs and teasing. But this time, her sobs only slowed slightly.

She sniffled as she turned her head toward me. Her eyes glistened with tears, the skin around them red and puffy. God, this one wasn't good. I knew she shouldn't have gone on that date. That boy was trouble from the beginning. I knew he would let her down. I knew it, and yet I could do nothing to stop her from going.

I swallowed as she met my gaze with trembling lips and tears stained on her rosy cheeks.

"Why does this always happen to me, Kadri?" She whimpered. "Why do I always pick the bad ones?"

I extended my snout and nudged her cheek, pushing aside more wet hair. She sniffled, but let me nuzzle her. Good, she wasn't pushing me away. She was saddened—but not angry this time.

I eyed her, letting her catch her breath before I tilted my head. *What happened?* I wanted to ask. But she always seemed to understand me, even if I couldn't speak to her in her own tongue.

She let out a shuddering breath. "He was late. I arrived at the café, ordered a coffee, and sat at a table waiting for him for over an hour. I got all dolled up, and while I was waiting, I did my makeup all cute. I even did my hair for him!"

I nodded slowly. She liked to dress up, and she liked to appear cute and pretty on a daily basis. But her long, crimson hair, hanging nearly to her hips, was a whole other story. She usually threw it into a bun or a ponytail just to get it out of the way.

I had laid my body on the floor just outside the bathroom mere hours ago while she sang to her favorite songs that blared from the radio, while painstakingly curling and bouncing her hair. She left the house in a flowy red sundress that shined against her fair skin, black wedges to add some height to her small form, a bag full of makeup to paint her face with because she always got to these dates early, and red curls bouncing around her shoulders. She had grinned at me as she left, that hopeful, eager smile gleaming. Now, it was a wobbly, tearful mess.

I lifted a paw and gently laid it atop her hand. She smiled tightly and brushed a thumb over my fur, but the curl of her lips was forced.

"I got there early like I always do, did my makeup, drank my coffee, and even read through a magazine that was on the table. But then ten o'clock came and went, and Logan didn't come." She sniffled. "I thought he might not show, but then almost an hour and fifteen minutes later, he rushed through the door. And I-I was so happy that he even came at all that I shrugged off his tardiness."

I kept her gaze even if I wanted to shake my head. She shouldn't have stayed. She shouldn't have waited for a man who didn't respect her time or commitment. That was a red flag—why did she always ignore those?

"He apologized over and over, saying he had car trouble and had to take his bike instead, and I just waved him off. It was fine, and things happen. No big deal. I was just happy that he came at all, and we could hang out and enjoy our time together."

But...

"Things were good at first. He ordered a coffee and a sandwich, we talked and joked, and he told me about the upcoming vacation he planned to go on with his friends. Apparently, his guy friends and himself were planning to go to the islands for a long weekend. They were going to rent hotel rooms and already had everything lined up in their itinerary. And then he said his friends were all going to bring a girl with them. Some had girlfriends while others were bringing hookups or even just casual female friends."

Ah, I nodded in understanding. *This is where it all went wrong.*

Scarlett sniffled, a harsh sob choking her. But she pushed on through her tears and wobbly voice.

"It all sounded so luxurious and fun and—you know, I haven't been to the islands before. So, I asked him if he was bringing a girl, too. He said he was, but he still had to ask if she wanted to come. We had been on four dates, and his smile at me made me all warm and mushy inside. He had to ask me to come, right? Of course, he'd ask me."

Scarlett's composure snapped as a sob raked through her. "No. He didn't want to ask me to come on this luxurious vacation. He didn't want to ask if I was even interested. He only wanted to meet up today to tell me that he was going on this vacation with another girl, who, apparently, he has been seeing recently. One whom he has gone on two dates with and *really feels a connection with.*"

Oh, no... Scarlett—

Tears streamed down her cheeks as her nose leaked. She gasped for breath as choking sobs coursed through her. I turned for only a moment to pick up a tissue box with my mouth. I set it in front of her and nudged her hand to grab a tissue. She did and blew into the fabric with the force of a trumpet. I flinched.

"Logan dumped me. Just flat out dumped me for this new girl whom he has already decided is 'the one' and wants to go on this trip with instead. And then... and then..." She choked on a forced breath. I leaned my furry head on her hand and urged her to finish. "And then he just got up and left, leaving me to pay for his meal, too. And the icing on the cake? The girl he's seeing picked him up in her car. Yeah, he threw his bike in the back of her car, hopped in the passenger seat, and *waved* at me through the window as they drove away."

I couldn't stop the growl from escaping me this time. How *dare* he? How inconsiderate of another person's feelings does someone have to be to be that blind? That *immature*? I nuzzled my nose into the crook of her neck as her sobs took over once again.

Scarlett, it's okay. It'll be okay. That guy—he's a jerk, and you deserve so much better. This will pass. It's okay, Scarlett—

I nuzzled and purred against her, trying desperately to pass my warmth, my love, through her. She needed it—she *always* needed it. Because while Scarlett Dempsey was strong, proud, and passionate, she had been knocked down again and again and again. The men she surrounded herself with were callous and selfish. They took advantage of her kindness and the care she put forth to everyone around her, everyone she cared about. She was trusting, open, and willing to give anyone and anything a second chance. But these men... they didn't deserve it.

They didn't deserve *her*.

She wrapped her arms around my neck and squeezed herself close. Her red, splotchy face pressed against the fur of my cheek. Her tears soaked into my fur, but I ignored them for now. I would clean myself later. For now, Scarlett needed my attention, my presence, and my care. Something no other person in her life had given her.

I nuzzled my wet nose deeper into the curtain of her hair and pressed it against her neck. I purred, vibrating with warmth and love for this girl before me. She had cared so much, so deeply, from the very beginning.

For every new man who entered her life, she wiped the board clean and tried again. Every time, she started with a blank slate, and every time, they hurt her. Only for her to come home in tears, crying over a man who hurt her yet again. Who let her down, who dropped her and dumped her when they found someone else who captured their interest. This perfect, loving, and gentle woman before me was hurt, and every instinct in my body told me to alleviate her ache.

But how? I could give her company; I could nuzzle her and lick away her tears with my own kisses. But that was temporary. She would welcome my help and my presence; she would cry as she hugged me and wished for better things, better people—better men in her life.

And then, days would pass, maybe even weeks, and she'd find someone new to alleviate the hurt. She would forget all about what she went through. She would jump head first into a new relationship with the promise that this one would be different. This one would be real. This one would be the last.

It never was. And inevitably, it failed, too—*they* failed her, too. And she'd come running through the door with tears in her eyes, only for me to comfort her again.

It wasn't fair to Scarlett. It wasn't fair to me.

She deserved better. And if only I weren't this animal—this furry pet of hers—I could help her. If my words weren't lost in growls and grumbles, I could talk to her however she needed. If my touches weren't contained to only nuzzles and nudges, I could comfort her however she wanted. If my soul wasn't confined to this vessel of fur and stripes, I could be the man she always hoped for.

And idea then sparked in my head as a vague memory of an overheard conversation trickled into my mind.

One summer afternoon as I lounged on the upper floor balcony of our house, I overheard two girls talking outside. They were young, maybe in high school at the time, and sat together on a bench just off the sidewalk of the dirt road.

"Come on, Bethany! Aren't you even a little intrigued that there may be a witch living in the swamp?"

A witch—? I perked up.

The other girl sighed. "Not really. Witches aren't real, Alex. And I don't feel like wasting a whole afternoon trekking through mud to find nothing."

Alex huffed at her. "But what if she *is* real? She could use her magic to grant us whatever wish we want, just like Julia!"

"Julia was lying. She just wants the attention."

"That's beside the point. And even if Julia was just looking for attention, that doesn't explain Connor, Louis, Jacob, and Melanie all having similar experiences."

Bethany was quiet. I peeked through the railing, trying to get a better look. And just when I thought the girls might have left with the lingering silence, Bethany let out a long, defeated sigh.

"What do you even want from this supposed witch?"

"Um, I'm pretty sure you know what I'd ask for."

Bethany's tone *sounded* like she was rolling her eyes. "For Josh Martin to ask you to the dance, right?"

Alex squealed. "He's just so—!"

"Yeah, yeah, perfect and dreamy and so *cute!* I've heard it a million times."

Alex shoved at her friend. "Okay, then what do *you* want?"

"*I* don't even think she's—"

"If she *is* real."

Bethany paused for a moment, and with her pause, my mind wandered, too. A witch… living in our small coastal town? By the sounds of it, she granted wishes. If I could wish for one thing…

I looked over my shoulder at Scarlett, lounging on the sofa just inside the open door. She typed away happily on her laptop, probably talking to some new man who would only hurt her again. I flopped my head forward and set my snout on the railing. If I had one wish that a witch could grant me without question—it was easy, really. I wanted to be someone Scarlett could count on. I wanted to be a man whom Scarlett could lean on, and I wanted to show her how worthy of true love she really was.

I sat there and listened to the girls' conversation until they eventually got up to leave. In that time, I learned more about this supposed witch. She lived on the edge of the swamp, where nobody wanted to go near or intrude upon. They said the witch was fickle, and her wishes weren't granted for free. She demanded that something be taken if something else were to be given.

By the time the two girls were leaving, Alex had whole-heartedly believed that the witch was real and wanted to pay her a visit, while Bethany had dragged her friend away in the opposite direction of the swamp.

There was no way of knowing if the witch was real or not, but without other options available, I decided then and there to go find her myself. And truthfully, I didn't know where to begin, considering I hadn't left the boundaries of the house in years. Sure, Scarlett took me for regular strolls around the woods behind the house—where nobody would bother us or question the fact of a single woman living alone with a pet tiger under her roof.

But our strolls never extended into town, never even

grew close to the swamp. I'd have to find a way to get there on my own if I wanted to try and put my plan into action.

Scarlett's sobs quieted, and her tears dried as her breaths came out of her in slow waves. *Good,* I thought, *she needs to rest and recuperate.*

I gently stepped out of her hold and nudged her hands back onto the couch cushions. I then dragged a blanket from the nearby chair over to the couch with my teeth. I lifted it over Scarlett's small form and tried my best to cover her with it. Once she was covered, and a look of peace settled over her face, I sighed.

Scarlett, it will be okay. I will always be here for you. Always, no matter what. I nuzzled her palm and let out a low, throaty purr as her thumb absently stroked my fur. That's when I decided for good. This was my time. This was my opportunity. And by the gods, I was *not* going to let one more weak-minded little man hurt the woman I cared so very strongly about.

I stepped into the room that Scarlett had set up to be an office. I pulled down the pamphlet on the corner of the desk, knowing it was exactly what I needed. A map. Scarlett had been looking at it days ago when she was trying to find the location of the next farmers market that was popping up. It had moved from the year before, and she needed a little help remembering where exactly the street was that it was being held on.

I grabbed the corner of the map with my teeth and yanked it onto the floor, where I gently unfolded it as best I could, trying not to use my claws but failing in some spots where the paper caught. I glanced over the colorful paper, memorizing streets, landmarks, and geographical features of the small town. My eyes flickered over the map searching... searching... until—

There!

At the corner of the town and closest to the largest inlet that created the peninsula that the town sat on, was the swamp. *DeBonis Marshland,* was what it was called here, but I knew the locals all generally called it the *swamp.* My eyes glazed over the marshland, searching for any kind of features or landmarks there, but there was nothing. Nothing was mapped past the line that marked the marshland. Nothing was supposed to be there.

Making it the perfect place for a witch to hide away from the peeping locals.

I took mental snapshots of the map and created my own mental route to the swamp. Once satisfied with my plan, I stepped back out into the living room and took one final look at Scarlett. She was sound asleep on the couch and breathing slowly. My jowls pulled at the sides, eliciting the slightest hint of a smile that I could in this body. I gave her palm one final nuzzle before stopping at the front door. I flicked the handle down with one large paw and pushed the crack in the door wider.

Glancing over my shoulder, I gave Scarlett one more look as I stood in the doorway.

I'll be back, Scarlett. And when I return... you won't ever have to feel unloved again. Not one more tear. I promise.

With that, I stepped outside and pulled the door shut again behind me, hooking my paw around the flat handle. I stepped out into the bright sunlight, streaming through the wide leaves overhead. I squinted at the light, stretching my paws on the warm stones leading to the front door.

My bodily instincts had me wanting to spread out in the rays of sun shining through. To bathe in the light and relax against the warm stones. But I pushed aside that instinct and followed the stone path to the roadway. It was a dirt road, tucked away behind thick trees and the even thicker woods, but Scarlett and I liked it that way. We were hidden back here, with a quiet space to call our own from the hustle and bustle of the town.

I stretched my limbs as I started down the road and put one paw in front of the other as I made my way to the edge of town and the line of the marshland. After what seemed like hours of walking, hiding, and lurking just out of sight of some locals, and then walking some more, the landscape shifted.

Tropical trees turned to draping limbs. Big, wide leaves turned to vines and creeping branches. Grass shifted to mud and moss. And all traces of the town and its people disappeared. It was quiet out here. The birds chirped and sang their choruses high up in the trees, and little animals shuffled and shifted in the bushes. But I was alone. Completely and utterly alone until I drew upon a shack.

It was tucked between the crook of two large, willowing trees. Its wooden panels were cracked and warped with age, and most likely from the moist air surrounding the swamp. A large, and poorly maintained, stone path led to the front door. I took a breath before stopping at the pink painted door.

The witch is real. This is it.

I lifted my paw to rap on the door, but a voice from inside cut me short.

"Just come in; you don't have to knock."

I pushed the door inward, and it gave without hesitation. I peeked my head inside and found the interior as old, warped, and natural as the exterior. It was a cute little cottage, like something out of a nursery rhyme. An old woman sat knitting at the lone table sitting just inside the kitchen. She didn't even look up as I stepped inside.

The door shut behind me with a mind of its own. I whirled at its click, muscles tense and my body ready to fight or flee. But the woman chuckled and set down her needles and string. Her ocean blue eyes met mine, and she smiled, her teeth as crooked as her broken glasses.

"Well, well. Who do we have here?" She croaked.

I swallowed once before I stepped forward into the witch's kitchen.

2

"So, you want to turn into a human so you can keep your owner company."

I nodded once.

The old witch narrowed her eyes at me. "*Romantic* company."

Then it was my turn to blink at her. *I never said that. I just want to be there for Scarlett. To support her, to comfort her, to cherish her like she deserves.*

The old crone snickered, pouring herself another mug

full of hot tea from the kettle on the table. She had talked to me now for an hour, knowing exactly what I wanted and letting me explain why I wanted her help so badly. She didn't call me crazy, nor did she question why a full-sized tiger was in her kitchen in the middle of the swamp. She understood me, and she understood my wishes. Now, I just had to convince her to help.

She sipped from her steaming mug before setting it down to drip more honey into it. "What makes you think this Scarlett wants your love and attention?"

I grumbled low and throaty at her. *She's a living, breathing creature on this planet. She wants to be loved, appreciated, and comforted, just like everyone else.*

"Yes, but how do you know she wants that from *you?*"

I barely wavered, plopping my head onto the tabletop instead. *I am her loyal pet. I know everything about her, every like, every dislike, every dream, every hope and desire, every stressor, every song that she sings to, and what makes her cry. I know her better than anyone else. I've seen what these men do to her, and I will never repeat their mistakes.*

"How do you know?" She raised her gray brows at me from over top her mug.

Because I love her. I always have, and I always will. Scarlett means the world to me, and the last thing I would ever dream of doing is hurt her. I can take care of her; I can show her true happiness. She loves me already as her pet, so give me the chance to show her what my love can be like as a human.

The old crone wavered, setting her mug down gently on the wooden table. She wrapped her fingers along the ceramic, her long nails *clinking* in a melodic rhythm. I watched them, desperately sending waves of hopefulness out into the room.

Please, I thought. *Let me help Scarlett. Let me show her what she really needs.*

The crone eyed me before, finally, her fingers stopped.

"Alright, tiger. You've convinced me."

I jumped up, my head lifting in a spring of motion. *She's going to help me. I'm halfway there!* I nearly leapt with joy at her answer, to which the old woman chuckled at me and waved me back.

"I will help you turn into a human, but that is all I can do. Winning the heart of the girl you love is a task in and of itself, but that is one you must complete on your own."

I will! I absolutely will!

"But that's not all." She met my eyes with a stony hardness in her own. "In order to give you something, I must take something. Magic comes at a price and is never granted for free. So, if you would like for me to turn you into a human, something must be taken in return."

I barely gave her a second glance. *That's fine. Take whatever you want; it doesn't matter! Scarlett will see me for who I really am. Finally, Scarlett will be mine.*

The witch tilted her head at me. "You're willing to give up anything for this girl?"

I nodded without a second thought. *Anything.*

She shrugged and pushed herself up. "Very well. Then you, Kadri, shall be granted your wish. You will be given your humanity. And in return, Scarlett will lose her pet, her companion, and her best friend. That is my trade."

I huffed. Was she serious? Her trade was the deal we were making, anyway. If I became human, of course my tiger form wouldn't be around. That was a given. I nearly rolled my eyes at the old woman. How silly of her, wasting such a trade for something so obvious.

I lifted my head and met her gaze as she smirked at me with those crooked teeth. She waved me into her living room, and there I saw the altar before her fireplace. Bottles with unknown mixtures and poultices sat on every surface, herbs dried and fresh laid on slivers of fabric, ropes tied in knots with winding threads laid about, and a thick book sat in the middle of it all.

The woman groaned as she sat on the floor before the fireplace. She pulled out a match and held it over the logs inside, and almost instantaneously, the logs sprung up with a full, roaring fire. I winced, my instincts sensing the magic lingering and swelling within this room.

She then pulled the book closer to her, resting it on the edge of the stones. She flipped page after page until she stopped on a dried, brown page with the corner nocked with a dog ear. She ran a crooked finger down the script until she stopped on a block of text. She whispered at first, her words soft and gentle until they swelled with volume as her energy arose. The magic swelled with her and moved around her in waves—pulsing in and out, and in and out again.

Something in my chest swelled with it, sensing—*feeling*—the energy prickle the skin under my thick fur. I reared back a step as the crone chanted in tongues. She closed her eyes, lifted her hands, and crushed some kind of herbal concoction between her fingers. She sprinkled it over the book and finished with a final crack of the book's spine as she threw it closed.

I stared at her in wonder, feeling the magic energy sizzle out and dissipate all around me. But when I tilted my head to lick down my raised fur, I found my tongue to be short and my skin to be... bare.

My eyes widened before I raced to the edge of the room, where a mirror hung on the wall. I teetered off balance on two legs and nearly toppled over nothing, but as my hands slammed into the wall on either side of the mirror, I looked up. There, staring back at me with those same hazel eyes, but with a face made of golden skin, high cheekbones, a chiseled jawline, and dimpled cheeks... was *me*.

A human.

My lips curled into a wide grin, and each one of my pearly white teeth glimmered in the light. I touched my face slowly, my fingers feeling and curling around each of my features until I stopped to stare at my fingers themselves. I didn't have to bat anything with my paws anymore, or get frustrated with my inability to move or do anything with my limbs. I had *fingers!*

A loud, crackling laugh thundered through me, and the sound made me laugh even more. My voice… it was deep, rich, even if it cracked with little use.

A throaty chuckle echoed from the center of the room where the witch sat, smirking at me. I turned my wide gaze to meet hers. She studied me, her eyes slowly evaluating her work.

"Not bad. This Scarlett should be more than thrilled to see how… pleasant-looking her companion has become."

I grinned at her, taking one more look at myself in the mirror before stepping away. It was in that moment that a warm breeze drifted in from the window and made my bare skin crawl and tingle with chill. I glanced down. That was when I finally realized what the woman had studied so intently. The male human body was… strange to see naked. It was so bare… so vulnerable.

"Um, do you happen to have any extra clothes?" I croaked out, grabbing the nearest pillow to cover my lower region.

The woman pushed herself up with a laughing groan and made her way down the hall. "Now you're bashful, huh? I think I have a few large t-shirts and maybe a pair of sweatpants you can borrow." And just as promised, she returned with them in her hands.

I took them eagerly and stepped into the bathroom off the main room to change. When I stepped out again, I felt odd being so covered up. It was so unusual, so stuffy. Fur was much more breathable.

"Need anything else before you go?" the woman asked as she made her way back into the kitchen.

I followed a few steps behind, still gazing wondrously at my fingers. They were so long, so sleek. Nothing like those big paws—

"I don't believe so." I managed to get out, my voice steadily becoming stronger.

The woman plopped back down in her seat and grabbed her needles and thread. "Good, then get to it. I hope this Scarlett is happy with your decision. And I hope it was worth it."

I gave her one final glance as I stopped in the doorway to the outside.

"It will be. I know it."

The witch nodded and waved me off. "Off you go to woo your girl."

"And woo I shall." I grinned.

She shook her head, a breathy chuckle pushing at her lips. I laughed, too, and stepped outside, eager to get back home. To get back to Scarlett. I didn't want to spend one more moment away from her. Besides, I had been gone too long. She might start to worry when she wakes up alone.

I rushed back home, following the mental route that I had created in my head.

However, this time, the journey was much faster as I didn't have to avoid people's gazes and hide from the locals. I even waved to them this time around, and most of them waved back with smiles of their own.

But that wasn't where my attention laid. As I trotted up the dirt road and turned onto the stone pathway that led to our house, every nerve, every muscle, every fiber of my new body tingled and pulsed with excitement.

I lifted my hand to knock on the front door, even though I knew Scarlett would have kept it unlocked. She always did. But as I moved my fist forward, the door flew open from the inside. That was the first time I met Scarlett eye-to-eye—being not at the height of her waist, but nearly a head taller than her. She glanced up at me, her eyes red rimmed and her cheeks still splotchy. But as she met my gaze, her eyes widened.

"Um, sorry. Can I help you?" she murmured, clearing her throat.

I had to shake myself to respond. I coughed to clear the last bit of phlegm from my throat, too.

"Are you Ms. Scarlett Dempsey?" I asked, feigning innocence.

Her eyes flicked across my face. "Yeah. Who are you?"

"I'm Kadr—" I paused, making her lift a brow in question. I cleared my throat one more time and gave her the smoothest smile I could muster. "I'm Kade. It's nice to finally meet you."

3

Scarlett raised a brow, her eyes flickering over my face. "I'm sorry, but do I know you?"

I paused; a flickering pain in my chest surprised me. I knew she wouldn't recognize me. I was human, after all, not her pet tiger. But part of me still… hoped. I was with her every day, through every breakup, every holiday, every celebration, and every fit of tears. I was at her side for all of it. Now, to see her eye-to-eye—to stand face-to-face with her with nothing but opportunity in front of us—I found a hurt lingering in my core.

She didn't recognize me. She wouldn't, but it still hurt.

I lifted a hand and scratched it through the back of my hair, a chuckle escaping my lips.

"Well, no, um, I guess you wouldn't. I'm… new."

"New?"

"Yes! I… was born and raised in this town, you see, but once I turned ten, my parents moved us all away, and I've just recently moved back again."

"Okay…" Scarlett's questioning look didn't falter. "Did we know each other before you moved or something? I don't recognize you."

My thoughts raced as I looked at her. I had to control every fiber in my body from just jumping forward and pulling her into a tight hug. I wanted to feel her against me, I wanted to hold her warmth in my arms, and I wanted to comfort her after everything she had been through. But we were strangers. Scarlett didn't know Kade. So, I had to feign the innocence of a perfect stranger.

"We did have some clubs together in elementary school, but I wasn't very talkative, and I don't expect you to remember that." I laughed easily, but Scarlett only stared. She's not buying it. I needed to move on. "Anyway, I'm in town again, and after meeting with some old friends and talking, I was reminded of you. So, I thought I'd pay a visit."

"Oh," she wavered. "I don't… remember you well. Sorry."

I waved her off, my hand flying a little too far toward her. I still needed some practice with these new limbs.

"Hey, like I said, I don't expect you to. I just—" An idea struck me like a bolt of lightning. "I was hanging out with my old friends, and they mentioned your name after Logan said he had just broken things off with you—"

Scarlett's eyes widened at that. "You're friends with Logan?"

I huffed out a dry laugh at that. "I am, or I was. We aren't the closest in our group. And frankly, after hearing how he treated you with his whole vacation plan and everything, I don't even really want to be his friend anymore."

"Oh..." Scarlett took a step forward, standing in the sunlight that shone through the thick leaves above. I took this as my cue to continue.

"Yeah. I'm sorry about that, by the way. Logan's not the brightest, and he's selfish—always wants what he doesn't have. You know the type."

Scarlett shook her head slowly. "You don't have to apologize. It isn't your fault. I just..." Her voice broke with a dry, cracking laugh. "I always seem to pick the bad ones in the bunch."

I looked at her red face, her puffy eyes, and resisted the urge to pull her close. Instead, I took a deep, steadying breath and touched her shoulder. It was a light, gentle touch and nothing more. But I hoped it helped soothe her raging emotions.

"Hey, we all do that. It happens to the best of us. Right? And don't even waste your time on Logan. Like I said, he's an idiot, and you deserve a lot better."

Scarlett glanced at my hand on her shoulder, but she didn't step away or try to put any more distance between us. Instead, she—her lips curled into the smallest, sweetest of smiles.

"Thanks. I... I needed that."

"Anytime." I squeezed her shoulder gently before dropping my hand away. "So, um, anyway, it was good seeing you again, and I'm glad you seem to be doing well."

"Yeah, thanks." Scarlett's smile warmed as the evening sun made her cheeks glow.

I didn't want to go, and truthfully, I had nowhere *to* go. But I didn't want to overstay my welcome or make Scarlett question my presence here.

"So, I'll get out of your hair now. Just wanted to come say hi again after all this time." I smiled easily as the breeze ruffled my curly hair. I turned to leave, heading back up the stone path to the road. But just as I got a few steps from it and our house would have disappeared behind the thick leaves, Scarlett called out.

"Hey!"

I looked over my shoulder. "Yeah?"

She fidgeted with her fingers, her telltale sign showing her nerves. I felt the corner of my lips twitch at that.

"Do you have any plans tonight?"

I paused, giving the illusion that I was thinking over my schedule, before turning toward her again. "No, why?"

Scarlett's fingers squeezed around the fabric of her t-shirt. "Would you want to have dinner together? You know, to catch up and stuff?"

My lips curled into a bright smile just as my chest warmed with a flood of heat.

"I would love nothing more."

And so, that's how we ended up at a local café at the edge of town. We walked there together after I waited outside the house for ten minutes so Scarlett could change into better clothes. I didn't mind her t-shirt and leggings, and I told her that, too.

But she was insistent, as usual. She came back out of the house ten minutes later in jeans, a light and flowy linen top, strappy sandals, and with the barest amount of makeup on her face to cover the red puffiness under her eyes. I smiled at her and told her she looked pretty. She blushed then, but she didn't say anything more about her appearance as we walked to the café together.

We talked about the town, its people, the never-changing traditions, and her life and family. She talked about herself easily, and though I already knew everything that she told me about her life, I nodded and listened with eagerness.

She smiled when she talked about her job as a columnist at the local newspaper, and the blog that she was writing on the side. She laughed when she told me stories of her and her friends' adventures on the weekends at the beach and the surrounding coves. She gazed into the distance, her eyes shining and warm when she talked about her parents living on the other side of town with her younger brother, who was finishing up high school. And she glowed when she mentioned the very interesting fact that she had a pet tiger named Kadri.

We sat opposite each other at the table, sipping on our fountain drinks and nibbling on our sandwiches as she told me all about myself.

"A pet tiger, you say?" I shook my head with a chuckle. "That's wild. Isn't it hard to handle?"

She shook her head as she sipped on her orange soda. "No, he's calm and gentle with me. He can be a bit protective, and his instincts do take over when he's out and about with me on our walks. Sometimes he even sneaks out and disappears for a few hours on his own. I never know where he goes, but I assume it's in the woods behind my house. He loves wandering around there. It's probably the closest thing to his natural habitat."

I chuckled at that. She wasn't wrong; I *did* love the woods. It was nice to be alone and among the quiet of the trees. It was relaxing and replenishing.

"So, he wanders off, but he isn't hard to handle?"

She set down her cup. "No. He's independent, that's for sure. But he's never been difficult with me. He listens well, he responds to every emotion I'm feeling, and sometimes I even think he can hear my thoughts. That's how in tune we are with each other." She laughed.

It was my turn to shake my head, even though a swirl of pride bloomed in my chest.

"That's really cool. I'm glad you have someone so close to stay with. Kadri sounds like he really loves you."

She smiled at that. "He's my best friend. I don't know what I'd do without him."

But I could be more, Scarlett. I wanted to reach out and take her hand. To make her look into my eyes, to see the familiar gaze that she saw every day. To recognize me, to love me like she loved Kadri.

I took a sip from my drink to cool my heated thoughts. "I, uh, didn't see a tiger behind you earlier when I stopped by."

She nibbled on the corner of the second half of her sandwich. "Mm, yeah. He's on one of his wandering adventures now. I fell asleep after the whole debacle with Logan—" I couldn't stop the smile from slipping onto my lips. She already said his name like it's done and forgotten. She was comfortable with me. She was moving on. "And when I woke up, Kadri wasn't there, and the door was open. He knows how to get out on his own, so I don't try to stop him."

"Aren't you worried at all?"

She chewed her food without an ounce of worry on her glowing face. "About what?"

"Well, that Kadri might not come back? That he could get hurt?"

She waved me off with a laugh. "Kadri always comes back. He wouldn't leave me alone for too long. And have you been listening at all? He's a tiger. Nothing local here is going to try and hurt him."

I smiled, hiding it behind the lip of my drink. I took another sip. "I suppose you're right."

We finished our meals together, with drinks, stories, and

laughter flowing. Scarlett's sadness from earlier drifted away and disappeared into the night as we grew closer and closer. At some point, a band started to play, and the drinks switched from sodas to beers. I puckered my lips at the sourness of the beer. I hadn't ever had one before. But I knew at the first sip, it was not for me. How did humans drink such bitter things? And why would they *choose* to?

Scarlett laughed at my face and ordered us two coladas instead. As soon as our waiter brought them out, Scarlett sipped at hers eagerly. I stared at mine in suspicion.

"It won't hurt you," she laughed. "Try it."

"But the other one…"

She scooted my cup closer to me. "It won't taste anything like that. I promise."

I stared at it, not knowing what I expected to happen.

"Come on, you big baby. You'll like it; try it!" She laughed.

I huffed around my pout at her teasing. But nonetheless, I picked up the cold cup and slurped at the straw. A cool, baby yellow substance flowed up and into my mouth, and just as I pinched my nose, expecting the bitterness to offend my tongue again, a fruity sweetness came instead. My eyes widened as the sweet, tangy drink flowed over my tongue.

Scarlett's smile cracked wide open. "Well?"

I took another long sip, downing nearly a third of the drink.

"Slow down, tiger!" She laughed. I froze, but not because the drink tingled and numbed the front of my skull. "I know it's sweet, but it has booze in it, too. Go too fast, and you're going to regret it tomorrow."

"Why?" I slurped some more.

Scarlett tilted her head to the side as her eyes danced in question. "Have you never had a hangover before?"

I shook my head slowly, feeling the curls bounce around my forehead and ears. It was… an interesting sensation.

She snorted and took one more sip of her drink before setting it down again. "You're lucky, then."

Scarlett didn't tell me exactly what a hangover was after that. But she laughed harder and harder as one, two, three coladas went down the hatch. Before I knew it, she had paid the bill after I fumbled around my pants, only then realizing that I had no wallet, no identification, and no money to pay for anything. She didn't mind, though. She said it was her treat after getting to catch up with an old friend over dinner, which had been her idea all along.

After paying, we walked out of the café together. Well, I stumbled on my own two feet, and Scarlett acted as a giggling crutch as we made our way across the street and down the boardwalk to the beach. My legs felt like two numb popsicles with a mind of their own. Granted, I was still getting accustomed to walking on two legs instead of four, but this sensation was entirely different. How could I learn to walk on two legs if I couldn't properly *feel* my two legs? And when would my vision just… stop… spinning?

Scarlett crashed down onto the sand, pulling me along with her. She giggled relentlessly as I toppled over beside her. I barely registered the fall, and I felt no pain or the sand between my toes, a sensation Scarlett had mused about for years. Instead, I felt nothing but the cool, nightly breeze off the water, and Scarlett's warmth seeping through my thin shirt.

"I told you, you would regret it!" She giggled, pushing me back into an upright seated position on the sand.

I must have given her an odd look because she giggled even more at my gaze. Those drinks—what did she call them again?—whatever they were, were evil. Toxic, delicious, mind-controlling, sweet, amazing evil.

Without thinking, I leaned my head on her shoulder. It wasn't the most comfortable position, seeing how much taller I was, but I wasn't going to complain. I let my breaths come in and out in long, slow waves—just like the ones crashing before us.

I had never seen the waves up close before. Scarlett's house was further inland and up against the woods. She lived in one of the homes furthest from the water, and yet, that wasn't really that far to begin with. But it didn't allow us to see the ocean like so many others who had paid hundreds of thousands of dollars every year for a house on the water. Scarlett and I always preferred our peace and quiet over the beauty of the waterfront. But now, sitting here so close to the raging, pulsing ocean… I could see the draw.

Scarlett leaned her head atop mine and let out a long sigh as her muscles seemed to relax under her.

"Kade?" she whispered, her wobbling, giddy voice barely audible above the dark waves.

"Hm?"

"Do you believe in soulmates?"

I squinted at the water in the dark, my foggy mind desperately trying to make sense out of what she was saying.

"Maybe," I said slowly. "Do you?"

She didn't answer right away. But then—

"I do."

"Yeah?"

"Yeah," she murmured, her voice rising, ebbing and flowing like waves as she continued. "I think everyone has somebody. Somebody they were meant to be with—destined to be with—all along. I mean, everything has its perfect counterpart. The sun and the moon, the ocean and the desert, water and fire, earth and air, sadness and happiness—"

"Peanut butter and jelly," I murmured before I could stop my foolish tongue.

But Scarlett's body shook with her laugh. "Exactly. Everything and everyone has its perfect opposite to balance it and to keep it whole. You can't have one without the other. I think people are that way, too."

Her ideas rolled around in my mind, crashing and blistering the other foggy thoughts aside. Everyone has another—a pair.

"Who is your soulmate?" I whispered.

She wiggled her toes deeper into the sand and shrugged, making my head bob. "I don't know if I've met him yet. I hope to; I'm getting impatient."

I chuckled, that warmth from earlier creeping back into my chest once more. I knew who my soulmate was if the idea was even real. There was not one doubt in my drunken mind of who my other half was.

"I guess if I don't have a soulmate, though, the closest thing to it would be Kadri," she confessed. My heart nearly stopped beating as I felt her lips curl into a smile against my scalp. "He's always been there for me. He cares for me, he comforts me when I need it, and he's my rock, always on my side, ready for anything. He's the one being in this world that cares about me more than anyone or anything else."

She lifted her head then, and I lifted mine. We both looked at each other in the dark, and even though the moonlight was dim and the crashing waves drowned out most of the noise, I could see her eyes shine and her next words echo in my ears.

"I know he's a tiger, but if I have a soulmate, I think it'd be him." She chuckled then, her smile cracking wide open. "Isn't that just silly?"

I stared, longer than I know I should have. Scarlett loved me. She noticed all my care, all my attention. She valued my comfort and needed my presence. She loved me above all else in the world, and she knew my love for her was even greater. And now... now, I was—

Scarlett pushed herself up from the sand, only stumbling a little now. I tried to follow her lead, but my legs felt like sand in and of themselves. She laughed as she helped scoop me up as I pushed my legs as hard as I could against the shifting sand.

Together, side-to-side, shoulder-to-shoulder, and later, hand-in-hand, we made our way back to the house. I nearly collapsed on the wall beside the front door, and Scarlett giggled as she turned the handle and pushed it open. I gave her a long look, to which her bubbly, dancing gaze sobered.

"I can call you a cab," she suggested.

But I shook my head, pointing at my hip… or trying to. I had no money to pay for a cab. Realization dawned on her then, and her gaze flicked inwards toward the house. She hesitated for one moment, then two. I didn't want to push her; I could sleep outside if I had to. But the house was so warm and my clothes and skin were itchy with sand, and—

"Do you… want to stay over?" she whispered shyly, her fingers toying with her flowy top.

I nearly yanked her into a hug at that. Instinctively, my tongue wetted in my mouth as I would have given her a long, wet kiss. But I swallowed my saliva instead. That would be… inappropriate considering the circumstances…

"That… would be great, Scarlett. And probably for the best." I scratched the back of my head as I grinned. "I should have listened to you at the café."

She shook her head and stepped inside, where a light was flicked on. "Yes, you should've. Come on in. I'll get you set up on the couch."

I stumbled inside, using the wall to brace my weight. I plopped down on the edge of the nearest chair as I watched Scarlett gather blankets, pillows, an extra set of men's clothes —where had those come from?—and a glass of water for me. She excused herself to let me change and to change herself in her bedroom. I quickly made due with the new clothes, only tripping once as I pulled on the pant legs.

When she returned, she had on her pink and white polka dot pajamas with the shorts that climbed a little too high. I wanted to pull them down further; I always did. But this time, I found myself staring.

"Cat got your tongue?" she teased. I looked up and found her smirking at me from the back of the couch. She caught me.

I cleared my throat and forced myself to look away. "Sorry. I didn't mean—you're just so—well, you're beautiful."

Her cheeks reddened at that as her fingers flew to her shirt. "I'm just in my old jammies."

"Still," I murmured, an odd heat rushing to my own cheeks. For a moment, I thought I might have gotten a sunburn, but within moments, the heat dissipated.

"Alright, get some sleep. You're going to need it. My room is right around the corner if you need me, and the bathroom is right next to it if you need that. I filled your glass there and put an Advil beside it. When you wake up, make sure you take another, okay?"

I nodded slowly and sat down on the edge of the couch.

"Good." She turned toward her room but stopped in the doorway. "Kade?"

I looked over the couch to meet her glowing eyes.

She smiled. "Thank you for today. I… I had a good time."

My cheeks heated again, but I ignored them as I smiled back. Good. She deserved it. She deserved nothing but happy bliss.

"Goodnight, Scarlett."

"Goodnight, Kade. See you tomorrow."

With that, the lights were turned out, her door closed, and I was left alone in the four walls I had grown up in with nothing but my thoughts.

4

I awoke to something shuffling around me. It started out slow and quiet, but as I lied there, it grew louder, more desperate. I cracked my eyes open to search for the intrusion, but instead, all that consumed me was a raging headache.

An ache, furious and violent, bloomed and pulsed behind my eyes. It pounded against my skull, with each beat of my heart. I wanted my heart to stop so the pain might ease, too. I buried my face deeper into the soft fabric of the pillow. The

scurrying noises around me only grew louder—more inces-
sant. I remembered blips of the night before: the café, the
drinks—the sweet drinks—the stumbling, the beach, and
then falling asleep on Scarlett's couch.

I clenched my teeth so hard that my jaw popped as the
noises around me rang like sirens in my ears, making the
pounding in my head grow more enraged. I wanted it to
stop. I wanted the room to be silent. I wanted to be left
alone. I wanted this godforsaken headache to vanish—

I bolted upright, the nausea and pounding headache coming
right along with me. That's when, through squinted eyes, I
found Scarlett shuffling through her office. The door was wide
open, and books laid strewn about everywhere. My eyes shifted
to the living room around me, and that's when they widened.

Not only was the office a wreck, but the entire house
looked like a storm had rolled through the inside. I rubbed
my eyes, at first believing the sight to be a dream that I was
still a part of. But as my vision cleared, and reality came back
to me, sure enough, the storm lingered.

"Um… Scarlett?" I mumbled, my voice deeper than
before.

She looked over her shoulder for only a moment before
tossing yet another book onto the carpet.

"Hey. I didn't realize you were up. I'm sorry if I woke
you," she said, not a hint of apology in her words. She was
distracted, her hands fidgeting on anything and everything.

I scooted to the edge of the couch and tried again to gain
her attention. "It's fine. No worries. Are you, um, okay?"

She tossed a book over her shoulder and paused. I froze
just as she did and watched as she rushed to the window as a
car tutted by on the dirt road outside. She sighed and
resumed her digging.

"I'm fine. Why?"

"Well, you just seem… stressed about something." I watched her flip through a few more books before dropping them haphazardly onto the floor. Scarlett *never* disrespected books this way. She took care of her books like they were her most prized treasures.

"What do you mean?"

I stood from the couch and motioned around me at the mess. "Scarlett, we went to sleep in peace, and I woke up in the eye of a storm. What's going on?"

Scarlett dropped her last book and sighed. She gazed out the window in the office once more, and at the lack of movement, she stumbled into the living room. She plopped onto the chair opposite me, and her limbs sagged into the fabric like liquid.

"I just… you know how I told you Kadri always comes back from his adventures?"

I nodded slowly.

"Well, he didn't come home last night. I left the door unlocked for him and everything. Usually, he's back by now. He's never stayed out for this long before."

I could see the slight trembling in her legs, and the fidgeting of her fingers on the hem of her shirt. I wanted to tell her not to worry, that I was right here! But that wouldn't go over well, and if anything, she'd think I were crazy and kick me out on the spot. No, I needed to be patient, to listen, and be kind and understanding.

I moved to sit across from her and let out a slow breath.

"Do you think maybe he just found a nice spot in the woods? Maybe he decided to stay longer than usual."

She shook her head adamantly. "Kadri *always* comes home."

"Then maybe he just hasn't yet. Maybe he's just taking his good old time." I paused, a chuckle pushing past my lips at the irony of my thoughts. "Maybe he found himself a nice girl."

Scarlett surprised me when she jumped up. "Kadri is the only tiger around. Be serious! He could be hurt out there and needing my help!"

"Hey, hey—" I stood, too, and before I could stop myself, I pulled her into my arms. She was tense at first, tight and unwilling to relax. But as moments passed, and my hand stroked her back, her muscles slowly released their tension. "It'll be okay. I'm sure he's fine, and I'm sure he'll be back any time now. You said he's independent, right? So, don't worry."

Scarlett settled in my arms, her tight, shallow breaths slowing until they were normal again. Minutes went by, and she made no move to step away, so I held her. Greedily and maybe a bit selfishly, but nothing in my body would allow me to let her go now. That was, until she looked up at me with those big, brown eyes, glowing and twinkling in the light with unshed tears. A sight that clenched my chest tight every time.

"You really think he's okay?"

I pulled her to my chest and rested my head atop hers. "I'm sure he's just fine. I promise."

"How?" she murmured against my shirt.

"How what?"

"How can you promise that?"

I paused, stroking slow circles on her shoulder blades with my thumb. I let out a slow breath and felt her hot tears staining my shirt.

"I just... know. Kadri is much closer than you think. Trust me."

5

After a slow and quiet start to the morning, Scarlett finally started to brighten again. I took it upon myself to make her breakfast, though admittedly, I had never made any kind of food before. She eyed me when I pulled everything I thought I needed out of the cabinets in the kitchen, surely wondering how I knew where everything was. But I swiftly shifted her attention away when I pulled out a rubber spatula.

"Do you think I'll need this for eggs?"

Scarlett raised a brow at me. "A rubber spatula?"

I nodded earnestly. I tried to remember everything I had seen her use when she made eggs herself, but the rubber spatula made me waver.

Scarlett giggled, breaking the layer of tension that had settled over the room. "What, do you plan on baking the eggs? Perhaps put them in a cake or brownies?"

I pursed my lips at her, barely concealing the smile that was breaking through.

"Hey, it was an honest question!"

She full-on belly laughed, then. "Have you never made eggs before?"

I bit my lip. "I, uh… don't have a lot of experience cooking."

"Well, we must change that. Everybody should at least know the basics."

"And what are those?"

Scarlett pushed herself up from the stool behind the counter and made her way into the kitchen. She ticked off one by one on her fingers, "eggs, spaghetti, grilled cheese, and ramen. You have to know how to make those, at the very least."

I scratched at the back of my neck. "I don't know how to make any of those. I mean—I have some idea on how to, but… I would like to not burn down our house today." I laughed before I caught my mistake.

Our house? How could I be so careless?

But Scarlett waved me off without another look. "Then let's get started."

Eggs were cracked, pans heated, butter smeared, and after half a carton of failed attempts to flip the eggs with the yolk intact, Scarlett took over. She laughed as she flipped the first egg perfectly, and I gasped—followed by a pout—at her reaction. She turned on music at some point, and we shimmied and swung our hips while the eggs fried on the stovetop.

I recognized most of the songs she played, even if I wasn't totally used to using my vocal cords to sing along to them. Scarlett sounded like a sweet, chorusing angel while I... well, I would compare my singing voice to a whining, shrill cat with pneumonia. But Scarlett didn't care. She was too kind to point out my complete lack of tone.

We munched on our eggs and toast in silence, the music a calm beat behind us as we sat at the counter. Scarlett bobbed up and down on her stool as she ate, a sure sign that she enjoyed what she was eating. I smiled around my mouthful of food, not even savoring the new tastes in my mouth because of the bubbly, smiling girl beside me.

We finished up shortly after, and I helped her clean all the dishes. Once the kitchen was spotless, and the afternoon sun shone in through the balcony sliding door, we made plans to go to the beach. I had never been, aside from our little night-time escapade the night before. But whether it was my own faulty memory or the toxins of the sweet drinks I'd downed, I couldn't seem to recall most of our time on the beach.

Scarlett gathered up towels, an umbrella, and her music speaker while I got the sunscreen, sunglasses, and hats. Once our pile of beach goods was packed into bags, Scarlett ran into her room with a grin to go change into her bathing suit. It was at that moment that I realized I didn't have a suit of my own. I called out to Scarlett, telling her my realization, and she laughed through the closed door.

"We'll buy one from the beach shop on the boardwalk!"

"Oh, okay."

I settled onto the couch, holding the handles to both bags in my hands as I waited. Minutes went by in silence, and I found my foot bobbing on the floor in anticipation. Then her door cracked open, the hinges creaking. I looked over my shoulder as she stepped out in a tank top and denim shorts that came… very high up her thighs. She smiled knowingly when she caught my lingering gaze.

"Ready?"

I jumped up from the couch and rushed for the door. "Absolutely!"

We made our way down the dirt road to the main road leading into town. We walked block after block, easy conversation flowing between us. I knew that I had been in Scarlett's life forever, and that I knew every detail about her, but she didn't know that. She thought I was a stranger from her past. And still, her smiles, her laughter, her joy, unimpeded. It let me think that maybe—just maybe—I had a chance.

We stopped at the beach shop on the boardwalk on our way. Scarlett glanced over the t-shirts and sunglasses while I grabbed a dark blue pair of boardshorts with white palm trees on them. I paid for them—well, Scarlett did, and I added it to the list of things I needed to pay her back for— and ran into the restroom to change.

I emerged moments later, and Scarlett smiled at me, waving me toward the door. We stepped outside into the bright sunshine and made our way down the boardwalk and to the beachfront.

It wasn't terribly busy for a weekday, seeing as how most people were working or busy—Scarlett was off work every Thursday, a fact I didn't forget. Small groups of kids, elementary aged all the way to high school teenagers, roamed and ran across the sand. School was out for the summer, and the sheer unadulterated joy was not remiss. Scarlett looked for the perfect spot to put our belongings while I tagged behind at a distance. It was… beautiful here.

The sun shone brightly on the sand, warming it between my toes. The waves reflected off the rays of light, crashing and pulling and crashing again in a perfect tidal chorus. The seagulls ahead cawed and perched on benches, lingering close to the few tourists who kept their food a little too far outside their towels. Coolers marked the spots of families already settled, kids ran freely, laughing and squealing with delight. I smiled as I closed my eyes against the light, letting the warmth of the beach bathe me.

"Hey! Let's set up here!" Scarlett called.

I peeked my eyes open and found her standing some twenty feet away. Her hair blew lightly in the breeze, her smile cracked wide into a bright grin, her cheeks reddened from the heat shining down on her, and she held her wide-brimmed hat down with one hand as she waved me over. I smiled as I jogged to catch up.

I set down our bags and helped Scarlett spread out the towels with the rest of our stuff. Once she was satisfied with our layout, she grabbed the sunscreen that I'd left on one of the towels and turned toward me.

"Alright, you first."

I looked over my shoulder only half-jokingly. "Me?"

That earned me a laugh. "Yes, you. Get over here, and let me get your back covered up."

"I-I can do it myself," I faltered, becoming shy all of a sudden. Why didn't I want her to touch me? Was it because my shirt wouldn't be between us? Because she'd be touching bare skin and that… that was much more… intimate?

She snorted and yanked my arm forward so I stood before her. "You can get your front and shoulders, but if you argue with me, your back is going to burn. Didn't you learn your lesson with the drinks last night?" she teased, her brows raising.

I groaned as I turned around. "Yes, yes. You know all, and I need to trust your judgment."

"Exactly." Scarlett grinned as she fingered the hemline of my shirt. "Now, off with it! Don't be shy."

I turned to hide my blush as I slipped my shirt over my head. I swore I could hear Scarlett gasp—I *swore*—but when I looked over my shoulder, she avoided my gaze. Instead, clearing her throat and rubbing white lotion all over my back. I couldn't tell exactly what surprised her, but one look at my chest and abdomen, and I had a pretty good hint.

The witch in the swamp not only made me human—she made me a toned, muscular, and nearly *perfect* human. I flexed the muscles in my abdomen, and the individual abs twitched. I smirked and glanced over my shoulder again, only to find Scarlett's cheeks bright red as she rubbed in the lotion.

"Okay, all done. My turn!" She shoved the bottle into my hands as I turned.

I smirked as I took it and squeezed a dollop of lotion into my hands. But when I looked up, and Scarlett tugged off her shirt—and then her shorts—my eyes dipped shamelessly.

She was all lean and toned. She wasn't lanky like those other girls she always compared herself to in high school. She was stocky, sturdy, and solid. But that made her even more beautiful to me. She was fair-skinned, and her paleness made her almost glow in the sunlight. Her bikini hugged all the right curves of her chest, and then her hips, and her hair blew across her shoulders in flowing wisps.

My breath caught in my throat. But she didn't seem to notice as she whirled around to face away from me.

"Lather me up. I don't want to burn, either." She chuckled nervously.

I cleared my throat as I started to rub lotion across her skin. It was so smooth, so soft and warm. I had wanted to touch her for years, had dreamt of the feeling, even. And now… it was almost too much to bear.

"Wouldn't want that," I said, my voice coming out more like a croak. What was wrong with me?

After a few moments of rubbing in the sunscreen, Scarlett turned, grabbed the bottle from my hands, and began putting on the rest herself. I followed suit, my eyes wandering to her perfect figure. Once satisfied, Scarlett clapped her hands together and grinned, all traces of embarrassment gone.

"Ready for a dip?"

I took one glance at the water and winced. I wasn't necessarily afraid of it; I just didn't really… like it. I was a tiger before, after all. Water wasn't out of the question in my native habitat, but I had gotten accustomed to avoiding it, now in captivity. So, while the sun shone down on us with a warm, almost blistering heat, and the sand burned under my bare feet, I still didn't find the idea of a dip all too appealing.

"Uh… I might just sit this one out. I can watch," I suggested.

Scarlett tilted her head at me, her brows knitting together with her smirk.

"Oh, my apologies. I didn't know my new friend was *scared* of the water."

"I'm not scared!"

"Sure."

"I just… don't really feel like swimming," I asserted.

"In this heat? Yeah, okay. The only reason you aren't already in the water is because you're a big ol' scaredy cat!" she teased, her smirk widening.

I glanced at the water, and then back at her. It couldn't be all that bad, right? I was human now. I didn't have to clean myself like I did when I was covered in fur. I could shower. My skin could just be washed clean. And besides, it *did* look refreshing in this heat…

"Fine!" I ran past Scarlett before she could get one more poking tease in. I heard her call after me before footsteps sounded and laughing echoed over my shoulder. But I didn't stop to look. If I stopped now, I didn't think I'd have the courage to dive in.

I sprinted closer and closer to the water, and just as I reached the closest receding wave, the water trickled over my bare feet. I flinched instinctively, but then the coolness washed over my hot skin, alleviating the burning sensation in my feet right away. My eyes widened, and before I could question myself, I ran into the deeper water and jumped in so it covered my head.

It was strange, the sensation of being underwater. Scarlett had bathed me before in the tub when I got muddy during a particular adventure in the woods. But that was different. The water—the ocean and its energy—was all-consuming.

The waves rushed over my head one after another, uncaring that I was underneath them. The water reflected green and blue in the sunlight shining down through it. The rays of light scattered, creating fireworks in the water with bubbles rising up all around. Salt tickled my nose and burned my eyes, but I didn't close them right away.

I burst up through the surface and took a gasping breath of fresh air.

"Kade!" Scarlett rushed through the crashing waves a few feet away, the water already up to her chest. "Are you okay? You were under for so long; I thought you might have gotten sucked in under the waves."

I looked at her in silence, and once she stopped in front of me, my grin broke my face into two.

"It's amazing out here! I can't believe I never came to the beach before now! It's… it's… unbelievable!"

Scarlett looked at me with the strangest expression, maybe a mixture of something I couldn't quite place in all my excitement. But then her smile broke, too. It wasn't wide and toothy like mine. No, it was small, gentle, and surrounded by rosy, red cheeks.

"I'm glad you like it."

Without thinking, I stepped closer to Scarlett, too close to consider any sort of personal space. I looked down at her and felt her chest rise and fall against my own. Her smile faded to something serious—something intent. My own grin dimmed as I couldn't help but focus on her lips.

"Thank you, Scarlett. Thank you for bringing me here today," I whispered.

Scarlett took a deep breath, her chest pressing against my own. "You're welcome," she breathed.

In that moment, it was just us in that vast ocean of people, of energy, of water. Nothing else that had thrilled me mere moments before was important. Scarlett had my attention now.

Only Scarlett.

But the moment couldn't last forever, and Scarlett chuckled awkwardly as she stepped away. I didn't want her to, and I wanted to pull her close again, but that felt like too much. Too soon. Instead, she whisked up a slashing handful of water right for my face. I tried to block against her assault, but was too late as the salt water splashed my face.

She laughed as she splashed me again and again, and I chased her with splashes of my own. We settled happily in the water, floating among the lulling waves after our splashing assault ended, with both of us breathing heavily and spitting out salt.

After we were thoroughly shriveled from the water, we went back to our towels, dried off, and lied side-by-side on the sand. We listened to the kids run around us and the gulls screech as they flew overhead, but neither of us minded. We lied in silence, soaking in everything until Scarlett mumbled.

"I wonder if Kadri is back."

I glanced at her to my left and found her staring up at the sky through her sunglasses. A part of me understood her worry. I hadn't ever been gone this long, and she had a right to be worried. But another new part of me was… well, frustrated. I couldn't help the feeling when she mentioned my name. After all we had done together, the truths we had admitted and shared on the beach, the fun we'd just had, the company we shared, the touches, the hugs—

She still thought of Kadri. Her pet tiger was always on her mind.

I sighed to myself as I adjusted my position on the towel. "Maybe."

Scarlett was quiet at first. "Do you really think he's okay? I mean—"

"Scarlett, we already talked about this. He's strong, independent, and he knows the woods well, right? I'm sure he's just fine."

I watched her throat bob as she swallowed. "Yeah, I guess you're right. I just… worry."

I knew she did. I knew she would, after all. And in that moment, I realized something. No matter how well Scarlett and I got along, and no matter how much fun we had together, her mind and her attention would never fully be on me alone. Not with my tiger counterpart in the picture.

Not with Kadri on her mind.

I turned onto my side and smiled at her. "I know. Now, before the two of us either get heat stroke or fall asleep here, I suggest we get going."

Scarlett eyed me. "Where to?"

I couldn't believe I was going to say it, but before I could question myself, the words flew past my lips. "To find Kadri, of course."

She perked up at that. "Do you mean it? I mean… he's *my* pet and *my* responsibility. I don't want to put that on you."

I waved her off as I sat up and began to gather our things in the bags sitting idly on the sand. "You won't feel fully relaxed or be able to fully enjoy yourself until you know that Kadri is safe, right?"

Scarlett sat up also and nodded.

"Right. So, instead of worrying, let's go into the woods behind our—*your*—house and go find him. He can't be that far."

Scarlett glanced out at the water and its waves lapping on the sand before meeting my eyes. Her voice was softer, shyer than usual.

"Are you sure?"

I smiled as I squeezed her hand. "Certain. Now let's go before we lose sunlight."

Scarlett didn't waste a moment more as she hopped up and helped me pack our belongings. We were on our way to the house before I could second guess what I had just done.

6

As soon as we arrived back at the house, Scarlett and I unloaded our beach bags, changed into dry, comfortable clothes, and made for the woods behind the house. We walked, and walked, and walked some more. I stepped over crunching leaves, twigs snapping beneath my weight. Each little shuffle in the brush or rustle of leaves overhead made me look, but I quickly realized that my sense of hearing wasn't as sharp as before. While I was noticing this and looking for the sources of such noises, Scarlett's head swiveled, in search for her pet.

I stayed quiet at first, trying to think of a way to explain myself. Should I even tell her the truth at all? Would she believe it? I couldn't know for sure, and part of me was certain she'd laugh in my face before turning to look further for her pet. But what else was I to do? With Kadri, her pet tiger, in the picture… she would never fully accept Kade, the human. Then it struck me.

The deal with the witch. To grant me my humanity, she had taken away Kadri the tiger. I thought nothing of it at the time, but now I understood why it was a fair trade. Scarlett loved me as a tiger. I was her friend, her companion, her roommate, and so much more. The only thing I couldn't be was her lover. Now, I was human and capable of that, but in turn, she lost everything else she gained with Kadri. She wouldn't forget that.

She'd never forget Kadri. And she would never get over that loss, even with me at her side. Unless…

"Hey, are you okay?" Scarlett stopped suddenly and looked up at me.

I nearly walked right into her as I shook my head to clear it of the racing thoughts. "Um, yeah, I'm fine. Why?"

"You've been silent the whole time. Are you sure you want to help me look for Kadri? I know searching in the woods at dusk for a girl's pet tiger isn't really high up there on romantic dates." She flushed, fiddling with her shirt hem.

But I shook my head. "I don't mind. I just…" My thoughts swirled and pulsed in my mind, refusing to settle. "I want you to be happy, Scarlett."

She looked at me, and slowly, her lips curled into a smile. "I am."

"Truly?"

She nodded. "I know it's only been days, and I still have a

lot to learn about you, but… it's been fun. And when I'm with you, well, all my other worries seem to float right out the window."

I smiled at that. But then my thoughts whispered again. *She might be more relaxed with you now, but she'll never forget about Kadri. No matter how long you're together, Kadri will always come first.*

I swallowed past the lump forming in my throat and stepped forward again to avoid my thoughts that came forth with the silence.

"Come on, let's keep searching."

Scarlett followed suit, and we looked up and down the woods for what felt like hours. We looked until the sun dipped, and the shadows from the trees overhead made it near impossible to see farther than a few feet ahead.

"I guess we should call it for tonight. We aren't going to find anything now." Scarlett sighed.

We turned and started heading back toward the house when Scarlett's foot caught on something. She stumbled forward, a gasp slipping from her lips. But I was quicker.

I caught her in my arms and yanked her upright again. I couldn't see her face well in the darkness surrounding us, but I could feel her eyes on me.

"Thanks," she whispered. It was then that I realized my hands still held her sides. But instead of pulling them away, I squeezed her side gently with one hand.

"Be careful. I don't want you twisting an ankle out here."

I dropped my hands away from her sides, but I didn't want to let go completely, and it seemed Scarlett didn't, either. As we started walking again, she reached out, and the backs of our hands touched. I almost apologized at first, thinking it was an accident, but then Scarlett intertwined her fingers through mine and squeezed gently. I was thankful for the darkness then, so she wouldn't see my own heated cheeks.

We walked hand-in-hand back to the house, squeezing each other's hands and pulling each other upright when we tripped over things in the dark. Somehow, we managed to get back safely and without injury, but the relief was short lived when I caught sight of Scarlett's glistening eyes as she pushed open the front door.

I followed her inside and closed the door behind me.

"Scarlett? Are you okay?" I murmured as I watched her settle on the edge of the couch.

She played with the hem of her shirt again, her eyes staring at it but unseeing.

"I don't know," she sniffled. "I want to be happy, and truthfully, I am when I'm with you. You've made me happier than I have been in a long time, Kade. But… but—"

I sighed as I came to sit beside her. "But I'm not Kadri."

She looked up at me. Her eyes glimmered with unshed tears, and her cheeks were splotchy like she could break into sobs at any moment. My chest squeezed at the expression. I knew she was worried, and I knew she was anxious, but this… I didn't want the loss of my tiger form to make her… cry…

"Hey, hey, it's going to be okay." I wiped at the corners of her eyes with my thumb, brushing away a tear that threatened to fall.

Scarlett sniffled some more. "But how? I couldn't find him or any tracks of him showing where he went. He just—disappeared!" Scarlett collapsed then, and I pulled her into my chest. Her tears stained through my shirt as they fell, but I didn't care.

"How could he just leave me?" Scarlett continued, her voice muffled and shrill against the fabric of my shirt. "Doesn't he know how much he means to me?"

I ran a slow, gentle hand up and down her back.

"I'm sure he does, Scarlett."

"Then why?" She yanked herself away and looked me dead in the eyes. "If he knows how much I love him, then why did he just up and leave after all this time?"

I could have given her any number of excuses. He's a tiger; he's independent and needs to be on his own. He's a wild animal; he couldn't stay cooped up forever. He wanted to wander the woods because that's the closest to his natural habitat...

There were many logical reasons to explain away my disappearance, and truthfully, Scarlett would have to accept them with little other option.

But I knew. I knew that if I gave her some lame excuse, she wouldn't buy it. She loved Kadri the tiger, and even if she was forced to accept his disappearance, she would never get past it.

So really, I had *one* option; I had to tell her the truth. For her sake, for her peace of mind, and maybe to alleviate some of the guilt that had built up in my own heart.

"Scarlett, I have to tell you something, but... I don't know if you'll believe me," I started.

She looked at me, her tears slowing as she focused. "What is it?"

I didn't have a good place to start, so I went back to the day before when she had fallen asleep after coming home sobbing after her failed date. I told her everything from start to finish. How I had heard the two girls outside the house talk of the witch in the swamp, how her sobs made me feel hopeless and wanting to do more than just comfort her as a tiger, how I decided to go find this witch to help turn me into a human so I could do just that.

I then told her how I came upon the house again, about the things that were different as a human, and how all I had wanted all along was to make her happy and to see her smile again.

"I didn't want to be stuck in the house and just be able to comfort you when you came home crying. I wanted to do more. I wanted to be someone you relied on, someone you trusted and cared about, and someone who would never, ever hurt you the way those others have." I admitted. "I wanted to be more than your companion, Scarlett. I wanted... to be yours."

Scarlett stared at me in stunned silence. Her eyes had widened and teared up as I told her everything, but not one more tear had fallen.

"You... you *are* Kadri, then?" she finally whispered.

I nodded silently, giving her a moment to soak everything in. I couldn't know what thoughts swirled through her mind. I hoped they were of relief, surprise, maybe even excitement. But what I failed to consider was that she might not be happy to learn the truth. I had kept it from her for two days while she worried about her pet's disappearance. Maybe she wouldn't be happy to learn the truth at all.

I opened my mouth to say something—that I wasn't sure. But then Scarlett cut me off.

"It was you all along. Kadri... Kade—" Realization hit as the name similarities struck her. She even chuckled. "How did I not see it?"

I swallowed past the lump that settled in my throat. "I mean, a witch turning a tiger into a man isn't a common story. I didn't expect you to realize." I tried chuckling, too, to lighten the tension.

Scarlett's eyes found mine then, and her smile slipped into a serious face. "Were you ever going to tell me? This whole time, I've been worried—"

"I know. I know you were. And that's why I needed to tell you. I couldn't stand to see you upset any longer. And when you cried…" I shook my head, the guilt festering in my chest. "The whole reason I wanted to become human was so I could make you happy. I never wanted to see you cry again. But I didn't think about you crying for me."

Scarlett's silence unnerved me. My foot bobbed, and my fingers fidgeted just as hers so often did. But I couldn't stop as she just sat there and looked over me. Her eyes skimmed up and down and up again, as if she were looking for the similarities between the me now and the me before. Just when I couldn't take the silence any longer, she sighed long and deep.

"You'll have to show me where this witch is, you know. That's a secret you're not allowed to keep."

My eyes widened. "You mean… you want her to change me back?"

Scarlett's lips slowly curled. "No. I don't."

Everything in my chest that squeezed and twisted and tightened released all at once. I couldn't stop myself as I launched at Scarlett with open arms. I yanked her into a big hug and nearly started crying myself as I hugged her tight.

"Thank you, Scarlett. Thank you. I'm so sorry for keeping this from you. I—"

But Scarlett laughed as she pulled me in even tighter. "It's okay. I forgive you. But don't scare me like that ever again, okay?"

I nodded against her shoulder, too grateful to say or do much more. We held each other for what felt like forever, but neither of us tried to move apart. It finally felt like things had settled, and the happiness bubbling up inside me welled over as relief poured in, too.

Scarlett pulled back slowly and met my eyes again. "Getting hungry?"

My stomach growled in response. Scarlett laughed at that

and pushed herself up from the couch. She held out a hand and pulled me up, too.

"Let's get to it, then."

"To what?" I asked.

She stepped toward the kitchen. "Cooking dinner. You have to learn the basics, remember? A good foundation is needed to do anything else after that."

A smile broke across my face as I followed her. She was right. I had so much more to learn, but now, with Scarlett at my side, I was ready to take on anything.

The End

THE INFLUENCER

ENCHANTED WISHES COLLECTION

Bonus Content!

Previously published in the Wicked Wishes Anthology

THE INFLUENCER

VIOLA TEMPEST

1

" If you're seeing this, it means we should be friends. So, like my page!"

Alexis Day frowned and let out an annoyed growl, swiping to delete the voice recording. It wouldn't do. She didn't sound… cheerful enough. She stared at her cell as the video played again, smiling to herself. She looked good, her makeup looking *just* right; she'd made an effort, but it didn't *look* like she'd made an effort. The T-shirt she wore was a size too small for her frame, revealing just enough of her figure without being too much. Perfect for Shutter, the world's most popular social media platform and, really, the only one that mattered anymore.

Alexis just couldn't get the voice right. She sounded too desperate, and in fact, she was.

She hadn't jumped on the Shutter phenomenon quickly enough, sticking to her previous haunts, ones where she knew exactly how the algorithms worked and thought people would never abandon for way too long.

People hadn't deserted the likes of Click, Flash, and Chatter completely; she still got decent traction on her profiles when she turned her attention to them, but they were an afterthought. Shutter mattered. That's where the influencers hung out; that's where the money was made; that's where she belonged.

Alexis just had to figure it all out, and her frustration with the platform increased each day.

No, not with the platform. She loved it and marveled at its perfection. Alexis just hadn't stumbled on the magic formula, the way to turn her videos viral, going from a thousand views to millions.

The previous night, Alexis couldn't sleep. She'd aggressively swiped through her cell, studying the most popular videos, watching "How To" videos on Chatter, reading endless blogs, and found nothing to help her. She'd done *everything*. Tried it all, but nothing worked. Finally crying herself to sleep, Alexis had concluded that she just didn't have *it*, so she'd have to change herself.

2

She woke up with a plan. With her first profile, Alexis had tried to be herself too much, revealing more of the mid-twenties, single, bookish, and opinionated woman she was. That wasn't Shutter. Skimming through the videos she'd uploaded, she realized she'd plunged in too hard at chasing those trending videos instead of starting off small and building the perfect Shutter personality.

So, she deleted her first profile. It caused a stabbing pain in her heart at first. Her palms grew sweaty when she pressed confirmed when Shutter asked if she *really* wanted to go through with erasing her handle and all her videos. Alexis almost said no. Almost. Even though it made her neck muscles tighten, her mouth go drier than the Sahara Desert, she pressed yes, and let her phone fall onto the bed. She'd curled up into a ball then, sobbing over the wasted past months and thousands of lost followers.

But she had to do it. They'd come back, plus more.

Alexis then went to work, cleaning the tears from her face, showering, carefully selecting her too-small T-shirt and tight leather pants. They had to be the right color, the correct shape. She spent an hour in front of her mirror, getting her makeup just right, her hair stylish and messy but suggestive. Then, she got on her bed, lying on her stomach, working to find the perfect angle.

Smiling, she reviewed the video one more time, forgetting how many takes she'd burned through before settling on the perfect one. Alexis smirked back at her reflection, brown eyes twinkling, feet up in the air as she lay on her belly. That pose seemed to attract thousands of viewers without a problem. Sex sells.

"Okay, let's try this again," Alexis told herself, waiting for the recording to play through once more. "Bright, cheerful. Spontaneous. You've got this."

Holding record, Alexis took a deep breath, suppressing the butterflies in her stomach, and matched the smile in the recording.

"If you're seeing this, it means we should be friends. So, give me a like!"

Falling back onto the mattress, Alexis laughed, listening to her voice repeating the words. That last-minute change worked. *Give me a like.* Not desperate at all.

"Perfect," Alexis grinned, fingers flying across her screen as she added a few worthwhile hashtags. "I've got this."

3

Pangs of pain shot through Alexis' stomach as she reached for her phone. She'd stuffed it under her pillow after hitting publish, resisting the urge to stare at it as the notifications flooded in.

Or so she had hoped.

It's why she had thrust it to where she couldn't see it and went on her laptop instead, responding to comments on her other social media, flooding her posts with *LOLs* and a healthy modicum of emojis. The love her activity received definitely helped boost her ego. Her experience with Shutter so far has really knocked it out of the park, and Alexis reflected on the strength it had taken to delete her old profile.

She'd never erased a handle before. Never. In truth, she'd never needed to; she had the social media knack so many others strived for. Before the rise of Shutter, people recognized her on the streets a few times a week while she went out for a simple cup of coffee or while she was out looking for that perfect photo opportunity. Of course, she posed for selfies with her followers; they helped her handles spread across the world, reaching new followers to love her.

But Shutter didn't work that way.

Taking a deep breath and ignoring the pain piercing her stomach, she reached out with a trembling hand, plunging her fingers beneath the pillow and almost shuddering when they came into contact with the cool, smooth plastic and glass of her phone.

Closing her eyes, she pulled it free, her fingerprint unlocking the screen without her looking. A tear trickled down her cheek. *This is too much; I can't do this. What if no one liked it? What if no one's commented? Worse, what if I get a handful of pity emojis?*

Her breath came fast. Even with her eyes closed, the room seemed to spin. The pain in her stomach increased, a constant stabbing as it tried to flip around, battling with her intestines to escape through her throat.

"No," she whispered, her voice shaking. "I can do this. I can!"

Opening her eyes, Alexis opened the Shutter app and laughed. Tears flowed from her eyes, and she scrubbed them away so she could see her notifications better, laughing again.

She'd only posted the video half an hour ago, but it

already had 2,432 views, 500 likes, a bunch of comments… and she'd gained followers! Just 700 so far, but she crushed the disappointment; it *had* only been thirty minutes!

Laughing, she liked all the comments, chatting to her new friends, striking while the iron was still hot. All the blogs she'd read said to comment, to like, to interact, all to help the video spread and gain more traffic.

Alexis laughed as an idea popped into her head and typed a comment onto her own post for others to see. "Hey! I'm new here, so would you share my video, too? You're the best. Love you!!"

"Okay," she breathed, placing her precious device down on the mattress. "I think my stomach will finally let me have some coffee, maybe some fruit, and then?" She grinned, glancing at her phone as more notifications swept in. "More videos!"

4

Alexis wiped the streaky mascara from her cheeks, her trembling hands smearing it further as she stared in the mirror.

"Hideous," she told herself. "Loser with no talent. No one cares about you! No one!"

She tried to sigh, but a wet sob sounded instead, followed by more tears. In the corner of her room, where it sat on a charger, her phone pinged. Even though the noise made her heart skip a beat, she ignored it. It hadn't made a noise in well over an hour. Stifling her tears, she waited, fixed on a point in her mirror where she couldn't see herself *or* the phone.

"Maybe it's just something with the time zones," Alexis whispered, nodding as she spoke. "I'm on the East Coast, after all. Maybe I need to upload my videos later on in the day to capture LA and the rest of California."

But her cell remained silent, the deluge of notifications refusing to sweep in. Alexis sobbed again and leaned forward, her head touching the glass. "Why? Why can't I get it right?"

It had all started so well. Her new profile gained a steady stream of followers, her videos a healthy number of daily likes and comments, and recent uploads brought views in for her old work, too.

But then the raging river of notifications dried up. Her clips, still pulling off that look of a cute, girl-next-door sexy style she aimed for, stopped gaining views. Alexis tried more provocative clothes, jumped on the spicy trends, and went on following sprees of her own, hoping the profiles would follow back, but nothing helped. Every day, each new video pulled in a lower number until the one that morning finally broke her.

Alexis had worn her lowest cut top. Her shortest shorts. She'd flirted outrageously with the camera, performing take after take until she had it *just* right. It was her magnum opus, the greatest Shutter clip anyone could ever take.

In the four hours since she posted it, the video boasted less than a hundred views and a handful of likes, with even fewer comments.

She'd torn through the trending clips on Shutter, rage building, breath harder to come by, frustration making her chest tight as she poured over videos inferior to hers, created by users with less talent and looks than her.

Or so her anger told her. When the tears broke her rising hostility, Alexis realized the truth. All the other Shutter creators had more talent than her and looked better than her. Were better than her.

"Why won't they, why can't they, see the thought and effort I put into all this?" Makeup ran down her face, black tears running away from her red-ringed eyes. "Why can't they just feel sorry for me and like my videos?"

Her sobs faltered. Pity. That was it! A last resort, sure, but it could work! Alexis tapped a finger against her lip, studying her reflection. A mess stared back, but she could fix it a little, so it still appeared genuine but presentable. Dabbing at her face with some tissues had the desired effect, cleaning the worst of the wreck of blacks, blues, and reds on her face.

She hesitated, turning around in her chair, eyeing her maddeningly silent cell. Making people like her because they felt sorry for her… It was desperate.

Alexis smiled. "A pity follow is still a follow!"

She jumped to her feet, a bounce in her step she hadn't had since her Shutter triumph two days before, and grabbed her phone, yanking it free from its charger. She took in the notifications it had blared, a follow, like, comment, and private message from a user called DreamComeTrue, and hit the create icon. Taking a deep breath, she started to record.

"Life is just so hard, right?" Alexis wailed, putting enough of her true feelings into her voice. "Just nothing ever goes the way I want it to. I'm not pretty enough, so no boyfriend. Not rich enough, so I can't get the things I want. Now, no one will even leave me a like or a follow?" She let a sob leak from her mouth, and she didn't have to try all too hard to make it sound real. "What do I have to do? Please, tell me. Please!"

Bottom lip trembling, Alexis hit publish. No hashtags, no witty, suggestive comment. She sent it out into the digital world, and as she did, her stomach flipped.

Did I just make a mistake? Oh, no, I did, didn't I?

Bile flooded her throat. Sweat surged through her skin, making her palms slick. Her head pounded.

"Oh, God," Alexis wailed, trying to breathe normal breaths. "I'm having a panic attack."

Vision swimming, neck muscles tight, she glanced around the room, looking for anything to distract herself. Her eyes fell to her screen, the Shutter app still open, the private message from DreamComeTrue still waiting for her.

"That'll do!"

"I've seen your profile," the message from the anonymous profile read. "You've got talent, but you need luck to cut it online these days. I can help you."

Alexis bit her lip, the waves of panic subsiding a little as she focused on her cell. About to message back, the typing icon appeared below the message. DreamComeTrue was writing!

She jumped when her cell pinged.

"I'd delete that clip if I were you," the new message read, "though I get what you're going through. Users will just laugh at you, but I won't. I want to help, and I know I can. You listen to me, and you'll have all the followers you want. You'll be FAMOUS."

Famous. What Alexis had always dreamt about. People loved celebrities, obsessed over them, hung onto every word they typed, studied every photo and video they uploaded.

Alexis read the messages again. DreamComeTrue had it right; people *would* laugh at her clip. She pulled it up, wincing as her high-pitched whine of a voice disturbed the silence, her stomach flipping again as she stared at her tear-streaked, makeup ruined face and hit delete.

Tight muscles relaxed in an instance.

Returning to the private messages, she typed into her cell.

"Tell me more."

5

Alexis sat in a darkened booth of a local bar, The Exchange, a place only a few blocks from her apartment. A flicker of doubt had gnawed at her when she realized DreamComeTrue lived in the same city as her, but so did another twenty million people or so.

She didn't really go to bars, but this one opened early, and there weren't many people around. Jazz music thumped at an acceptable level, though it still made the booth's table vibrate. Despite being inside, and the bar's gloomy setting, Alexis wore her oversized sunglasses, and the hood of her pullover covered her hair and forehead. She didn't know why, but she'd done it on instinct. Dream-ComeTrue knew what she looked like; he'd seen her clips on Shutter. Sighing, she glanced at the time on her phone. The guy still had a minute to show. Any later than that, she'd leave. Doubt crept into her stomach again and whispered to her anxiety.

Alexis bit at her fingernails, the varnish chipping. She'd read about meeting followers, and every blog said not to do it. Any clip she found warned her against it. Stalkers. Obsessed weirdos. They preyed on the influencers, couldn't get enough of them, re-watching their videos, commenting with their demands, and searched the towns and cities they lived in for a glimpse of them.

What am I doing? I've come out here, alone, to meet a creepy weirdo called DreamComeTrue who says he can help me. Have I lost my mind?

"That's a nasty habit, you know? Biting your nails."

Alexis almost leapt out of the booth as her heart tried to escape through her chest. A man stood before her, grinning. Slim and average height, he wore a plain brown sweatshirt, faded-denim jeans, and white sneakers. His hair was slicked back, an expensive cut made to look accessible, and the faint smell of rich aftershave swam into her nostrils. His mesmerizing green eyes twinkled despite the gloom.

The guy screamed money.

"DreamComeTrue?" Alexis breathed, her hammering heart settling down.

"Call me Kel," he replied with a smirk and pointed at the booth. "Mind if I sit down?"

Alexis nodded, eyeing her cell. He'd arrived right on time. Kel glanced around, caught the eye of a passing bartender, and raised a hand.

"They don't do table service here," Alexis murmured as the worker approached.

Kel shrugged.

"Hey, how's your day, man?" Kel asked, raising his eyebrows and smiling.

Alexis stared at his perfect white teeth and his gleaming skin and wondered why she'd never seen such a beautiful face before on Shutter. A man like him would easily get millions of views with every upload.

"Good," the bartender replied, eyes shining. Kel obviously had the same effect on him as he had on Alexis. "What can I get you?"

Kel glanced at Alexis, then winked at the man. "Now, I've never been here before, so sorry about this, but I didn't realize you don't do table service... But could you get me an Americano and a Skinny Almond Milk Decaf Latte for the lady?"

He knows my drink... He knows my drink! Wait, how? Did I upload a video about it? I must have... Haven't I?

The bartender grinned. "Yeah, no problem. I'll make them myself."

Kel watched him leave, then turned his grin onto Alexis. She never wanted that smile to go away.

"So... You said you can help me?"

He sat back, crossing his arms, head cocked to the side. "Straight to business, eh? Being famous really matters to you, doesn't it?"

"Of course, it does." Alexis frowned. "I mean, look at you. You've got everything."

Kel laughed. "I'm not famous."

"You must be!" Alexis leaned forward. "You've got money for the most expensive clothes, you know, the ones that don't *look* expensive, but they really are. Your teeth are the whitest I've ever seen. Your skin doesn't have a single blemish. You can charm people into doing whatever you want… You *must* be famous."

The bartender returned, carrying the drinks and setting them down without taking his eyes off Kel, who beamed back.

"They're on the house," the man said, cheeks turning red.

"Ah, thanks," Kel replied, pulling out his phone. A high-end phone, just released. "Can I leave you a tip, though? It's only fair." The man nodded. "How much do you make an hour?"

"Ten dollars," he replied, pulling out an e-reader for payment.

Kel typed on his phone, then tapped it against the reader. "There you go. Have a nice day, my good sir."

"A hundred dollars?" the man cried, eyebrows shooting up his forehead. "I can't accept this."

"You can, and you will," Kel replied, his voice and eyes a little rougher than before. "Now, have a nice day."

He sipped at his Americano as the man staggered off, dazed by his good fortune, and winked at Alexis.

"See," she said, "you *are* famous. The way you tipped him and sent him on his way."

"Being famous doesn't bother me." Kel smiled, putting his coffee down. "Helping people does. So, tell me this; why do *you* want to be famous?"

"I want people to love me." Alexis didn't even need to think about it; the desire was seared into her soul ever since she grew up watching influencers living their best lives on Chatter. "I want to matter to people."

"And being famous makes that happen?"

Alexis stared at him. Didn't he understand? "Of course it does! Being famous is the best thing you can hope for. Why bother doing anything if people aren't going to notice?"

Kel tapped a finger against his lip, the shadow of a smile

on his face. Alexis blinked. The light surrounding him appeared darker than before, his green eyes brighter. She blinked again and shook her head, the man opposite her suddenly normal again—*just a trick of the light.*

He reached into his pocket and withdrew a small vial. Glancing around, he placed it on the table, letting it stand between them. A glittery gold liquid filled it; one Alexis couldn't pull her eyes away from.

"One sip of this will see your luck turn. Just a few drops onto your tongue, and your next Shutter clip will get millions of views. You'll get hundreds of thousands of followers. Loyal ones."

"Really?" Alexis asked, raising an eyebrow. She *wanted* to believe. The liquid glittered and swirled just so…

"Really."

She met his eyes. "What do you want for it? I've got money, but I won't do anything else, not until I know you better anyway, and that isn't a—"

"I don't want anything." Kel leaned back. His head cocked to the side again. "It's yours. My payment comes in ways you wouldn't understand."

I wouldn't understand? This is too weird. A magic potion? But what if it works… Alexis studied the liquid, the bar's lowlight playing off the glitter, soothing her. She reached forward, her fingers twitching. It could be the answer to all her problems.

"I can just… take it?"

Kel snatched it away from her grasp at the last moment. Rage bubbled in Alexis' chest as he held it just out of her grasp.

"Just a few drops at a time. That's all you need. Say it."

Breathing in, she let out a calming breath. It didn't work; her fingers still stretched for it. "Just a few drops."

"Remember that." Kel leaned forward and pushed the vial onto her palm. "This is potent stuff. Have fun now."

Kel climbed to his feet and walked off without a backward glance; he didn't even finish his coffee. The bartender looked hopefully in his direction and half-raised a hand, one that Kel ignored.

Alexis stuffed the vial into her pocket and snatched up her phone. It hadn't cost her anything, and just a drop of the liquid wouldn't hurt. Would it?

6

Weeks later, Alexis wondered what would have happened if she'd followed Kel's advice and taken just a few drops of the liquid. She hadn't heard from him since, though her private messages were hard to keep up with these days.

She hadn't followed his advice. Instead, she'd downed the entire vial in one go. Better safe than sorry.

Her limbs had trembled when the liquid slid down her throat, her stomach warm as it settled there, its sweet, peachlike taste lingering in her mouth as she smiled at herself in the mirror. Grabbing her cell, she put Kel's potion to the test and piggybacked on one of Shutter's latest trends. In all honesty, she hadn't expected much and tried to kid herself into nonchalance when she hit publish and set her phone back down onto the mattress.

The number of notifications she received drained her battery life within an hour.

Since then, she'd had to get multiple devices. Chargers hung out of every socket in her room, and Alexis pondered hiring a personal assistant to carry out all the pesky demands of being an influencer. It wasn't just on Shutter where her popularity had bloomed. Her presence across all her social media had exploded, and the advertisement money she'd made on Chatter would set her up for life within a month or two.

Grinning and leaning back against her new, expensive, and highly comfortable office chair, Alexis reviewed her follower statistics, pausing as she studied her Shutter profile. That had been the golden goose, the one that mattered more than any other. Before she met Kel and drank his formula, she had a measly three thousand followers. Now, she had twelve million people behind her, with thousands more rolling in by the second. By the end of the month, she'd be the number one profile on the app. People loved her. They hung off her every clip, imitating her, buying the products she suggested—which made her team of sponsors admire her even more—and creating clips in her honor, hoping, wishing, that Alexis would return the favor with a tiny like.

"Dreams *can* come true after all."

Glancing around, she picked up her burner cell, one with private profiles for her apps, one designed for her to take with her when she went out and about, a quiet cell that would keep her connected with the social world but not inundated with notifications. "I think I deserve a coffee today."

Getting to her feet and stretching, her eyes caught a new notification sliding into her DMs. Without thinking, she opened it, then scowled.

"Can we meet? Please."

It came from a profile called ShutterFlutter065. She'd already blocked ShutterFlutter001 through 064, the guy — and it just had to be a man — always asking the same thing.

The only drawback of fame, aside from the constant barrage of followers demanding attention, were the obsessives. *At least I was never that bad.* Hitting the block button and tossing her phone aside, Alexis pulled on a wide-brimmed hat and shades before leaving for her treat.

7

"Oh, my God… It's you, isn't it?"

Behind her oversized sunglasses, Alexis blinked at the barista who'd taken her order at Café Moon, her favorite local coffee shop. The girl's lips trembled, her hands shaking as she attempted to scrawl the fake name Alexis had given her onto the paper cup. *She must be new, never seen her in here before.*

"Who?" Alexis muttered, forcing her voice to sound deeper and huskier.

"Alexis Day, from Shutter!" the barista squealed, her wide eyes shining with unshed tears. "I knew you lived around here and hoped you might come in one day. I saw a Café Moon cup in one of your clips."

Alexis' eyes rolled before she could stop them, and she hoped the lenses of her sunglasses hid them enough. Anything could spark anger in an obsessive, their undying love switching to hatred in a matter of seconds. She'd seen other influencers talk about it before, the experience forcing them to tears while they recorded their clips, their loving followers sending them love to heal from the experience. Alexis had suffered it herself. On one of her rare recent excursions to the mall, she stopped to sign autographs in a shoe store. When she tried to leave as the crowd built, a young blonde-haired girl with big brown eyes hurled a swarm of abuse at her, calling her ignorant and accusing her of betraying the followers who made her who she is.

That reaction video still got millions of views a week.

Frowning, Alexis peered at the girl. She looked familiar, but she couldn't place her, though the barista's roots distracted her. The blonde showed through from her poor dye job. *Probably did it herself.*

"Sorry, I don't know who you're talking about. How much for the coffee?"

The girl's face turned to stone. *See, a crazy obsessive. I knew it. Sometimes I wonder if this fame is worth it... Ah, who am I kidding? Of course, it is.*

"Three-fifty."

Smiling, Alexis recalled Kel's way with the bartender back at The Exchange. It felt like a lifetime ago. "Hey, how much do you make an hour?"

The barista's mouth twisted. "Eight dollars."

Alexis' eyebrows climbed her forehead as she pulled out

her burner, typing away into it, then presented it for payment. "There you go, a little tip."

The girl took the cell, fumbled around with it as she grabbed the e-reader, then handed it back without a smile. "Your coffee will be ready at the end of the counter. Have a nice day."

Alexis' jaw almost fell open. She'd tipped the girl a hundred and fifty dollars! Fury welling in her chest, she almost pulled off her shades to reveal who she really was but thought better of it. People stood around her, waiting to order, cellphones in hand. A 'Do you know who I am?' melt-down would be all over Shutter within minutes.

Nodding, Alexis moved to the counter's end, her coffee appearing like clockwork. Grabbing it, cell glued to her face, she left, taking the long way home as she sipped at her drink, flicking through her apps, planning her new clips for the day, and wondering if she could somehow mention ungrateful retail workers. Sighing, she looked up, finding herself in a part of the city she didn't recognize.

Crap.

Her cell pinged. Frowning, she came to a stop. This cell never got any notifications. Glancing at it, her heart and stomach fluttered as one. It came from DreamComeTrue.

How?

"I warned you," it read, anxiety creeping from Alexis' gut. "An entire bottle at once is too much for anyone."

She glanced around. Did Kel follow her? The sun seemed darker, the shadows longer, the streets emptier. Pulling her hat lower, Alexis moved, head down, hoping she'd find somewhere she recognized.

Her cell pinged again. The anxiety worked its way into her chest.

"You should be nicer," ShutterFlutter066 had typed. "You mean an awful lot to me. To all of us."

Alexis' coffee crashed down to the ground and exploded onto the concrete as she ran. She didn't know where; she didn't care. Her body told her to flee, and her limbs agreed. Alexis ran, her phone pinging and pinging as notifications continued to flood in, chasing her all the way back home.

~

UNDER HER COVERS, Alexis trembled and sobbed, clutching her closed laptop, twitching as every one of her cells pinged and chirped. She'd turned them all off, but somehow, they powered back up and cried for her attention. ShutterFlutter's last DM, from one number 147 now, told her that she knew how she liked her coffee.

The barista.

Alexis wasn't safe.

Throwing open her laptop, she turned on some music — she didn't care what, anything to drown out the pinging — and gasped. Messages flooded the screen. Clicking into another browser changed nothing, changing apps didn't stop it, and the computer wouldn't turn off.

"I'm going insane!" Alexis laughed, tears streaming down her face, the constant pinging building into a hellish electronic cacophony. "I'm going insane!"

"Where are you, Alexis?"

"We miss you!"

"How's your day today, Alexis? You're my favorite influencer."

"I know where you live."

"Be careful next time you leave your house."

"I HATE YOU."

~

Outside Alexis' apartment, Kel shook his head and put his phone away.

"They never listen," he whispered, though he didn't feel sorry for her. He never did. "Enjoy the rest of your fame. I hope it's everything you ever wanted."

He melted into the shadows, the faint pinging of an army of cellphones sounding in his wake.

Viola Tempest is a dystopian fantasy and paranormal romance author who yearns to expose the truth of those in the modern world: the good, the bad, and the ugly. Her inspiration primarily stems from life experiences, those who annoy her, ex-boyfriends, and the crazy dreams that pop into her head every once in a while.

Enchanted WISHES

THE COMPLETE COLLECTION

VIOLA TEMPEST